Size
Matters

Size Matters

A Novel

Cathryn Novak

She Writes Press, a BookSparks imprint
A Division of SparkPointStudio, LLC.

Published 2016

Printed in the United States of America

Print ISBN: 978-1-63152-103-4
E-ISBN: 978-1-63152-104-1

Library of Congress Control Number: 2016943032

For information, address:
She Writes Press
1563 Solano Ave #546
Berkeley, CA 94707

Cover design © Julie Metz, Ltd./metzdesign.com
Cover photo © TK
Formatting by Katherine Lloyd/TheDESKonline.com

She Writes Press is a division of SparkPoint Studio, LLC.

This book is dedicated in memoriam to my parents,
Gerald and Charlotte Novak,
who taught me about the magic of words,
food and musical theater.

Table of Contents

Chapter 1: **The New Chef** 11

Chapter 2: **The Yellow Room** 16

Chapter 3: **John Frederick Takes a Hike** 19

Chapter 4: **The Plaid Flannel Business Suit** 22

Chapter 5: **Traveling Day** 26

Chapter 6: **Lexie's Bravery** 30

Chapter 7: **Aftermath** 34

Chapter 8: **Time Passes—Notes Part I** 37

Chapter 9: **Ribbit** 39

Chapter 10: **John Frederick and the Cancelled Breakfast** 46

Chapter 11: **The Silence** 50

Chapter 12: **Darkness, Light, and Marjoram** 53

Chapter 13: **Oolonging** 58

Chapter 14: **What a Beautiful Morning, Oh!** 59

Chapter 15: **John Frederick and *The King and I*** 61

Chapter 16: **The Heart Attack** 64

Chapter 17: **John Frederick Is Floating** 68

Chapter 18: **The Waiting Room** 70

Chapter 19: **Alien Abduction** 73

Chapter 20: **A Night in the Garden** 76

Chapter 21: **The Magic Room—Home at Last** 80

Chapter 22: **Chocolate Soup** 82

Chapter 23: **Brunhilde** 85

Chapter 24: **The Reverse Elf** 87

Chapter 25: **An Adventure** 91

Chapter 26: **"'Ome"** 94

Chapter 27: **Rags.** 96

Chapter 28: **Invasion of the Pod People** 100

Chapter 29: **Time Passes—Notes Part II.** 104

Chapter 30: **A Call for Help** 106

Chapter 31: **The Grandfather Tree** 109

Chapter 32: **Lexie at the Counter** 112

Chapter 33: **B. B. Bevins Comes to Call** 115

Chapter 34: **A Night at the Theater** 120

Chapter 35: **Colors and Confrontations (Epiphany).** 124

Chapter 36: **Gingerbread Magic?** 128

Chapter 37: **The Myth of Good Things and Small Packages** . . .132

Acknowledgments 135

About the Author 136

A large man with his hand poised above a plate of flaky

chocolate-filled croissants. A young woman with her hand

poised above an antique door knocker. And so it begins.

Chapter 1

The New Chef

*J*ohn Frederick is propped up on his bed, wrapped in what, in more formal times, would have been called a dressing gown. It is a dark-blue silk reminiscent of evening skies, embroidered in a vaguely oriental design. His laptop computer is perched upon his huge stomach like a warming hut at the top of an alpine mountain; a large white linen napkin covers him from chin to laptop. Though spoiling any possible hint of sophistication implied by the dressing gown, the napkin is a much-needed accessory, catching any crumbs that might spill from his hands as they travel back and forth from his mouth to the plate of pastries resting on a tray by his side.

John Frederick checks his e-mail with mixed emotions. He only gives out the address to a select handful of people: his business manager and a few top culinary experts. Yet despite this exclusivity, his inbox is, as usual, filled with spam. *Such a perfect name for this unwanted intrusion into his electronic environment,* he thinks, fancying he can even smell a disturbing odor of smoked meat and nitrates.

In truth, John Frederick much prefers communicating in longhand. It is his cherished belief that words written on paper have substance and solidity, and John Frederick is nothing if not a fan of substance and solidity. Words translated into pixels on a screen seem to him, by their very nature, to be more fragmented and ephemeral. He finds there is something inviting, and often challenging, about a crisp, clean sheet of paper the color of marshmallow icing, that embraces and holds the words.

John Frederick sighs. Downstairs Mrs. Floyd, his longtime house manager, is interviewing, yet again, to fill the chef position. It is a mystery to John Frederick why such a seemingly simple task as retaining a chef should be so difficult.

"My demands are so simple," he says aloud to himself with a sigh. "All I want is lovely, enticing food in sufficient quantities to sate my hunger." He communicates his likes and dislikes in clear, concise directions that should be easy to carry out. Is it his fault that the prior chefs were unimaginative, uncreative, and incapable of turning out the simplest dish to his satisfaction?

⊷•⊷

Lexie stands before the massive wooden door, the paneled entrance looming over her small frame. There is a heavy metal door knocker on the middle panel, and a rather incongruous-looking modern buzzer and intercom system on the adjacent wall. She brushes her hand against the worn brass of the knocker, but wonders if using this quaint implement might make her seem old-fashioned or behind the times. In any event, she knows she has little time to dither. It is nearly time for The Interview.

She takes a deep breath, reaches forward, and presses the ivory-colored buzzer. She hopes she can hear the response above the sound of her heart, which has turned into an enormous drum being beaten by a score of marching percussionists.

"Can I help you?" inquires a female voice rendered flat and scratchy by the intercom speaker.

"I have an appointment with Mrs. Floyd. This is Alexandra Evelyn Haynes."

Lexie stumbles only slightly as she enunciates her full given name. As always, it seems like too grand a name for a decidedly ungrand girl. Her parents, thankfully, quickly shortened it to Lexie, which—despite, or perhaps because of, its unfortunate similarity to "pixie"—seems to her to be so much more fitting.

I shall fit into my full name today. I am a professional. I am a chef. Lexie silently repeats this last phrase several times, like a mantra. Perhaps she is beginning to believe it. *I am—*

Lexie's chant is interrupted as the door swings open, framing an older woman, her gray hair styled in an old-fashioned bun.

The woman holds out her hand. "I'm Mrs. Floyd, Mr. Frederick's house manager. Please do come in."

Lexie recognizes the voice as a more rounded, less abrasive version of the intercom questioner. She nods and follows the woman through the large entryway. As she passes, Lexie can't help but glance at her reflection in one of the two ornate mirrors that flank the massive wooden door. It is not a reassuring image. *I look like a ghost: pale skin, pale-gray eyes, pale suit,* murmurs her inner critique. Even her crinkly red hair, pulled back in a hopefully competent-looking French braid, appears to have been transformed by her stress into something dull and lifeless.

Mrs. Floyd turns to the right, towards a slightly ajar door. "Please come in and have a seat." Once they've entered, she pauses for a moment as Lexie lowers herself into a chair facing the desk. "Would you like some tea or coffee?"

"No thank you. I'm fine," Lexie says, envisioning the brown liquid cascading down her lap and onto the floor.

"So, let's begin," Mrs. Floyd says. "Frankly, I was rather

surprised when I got your application. With such glowing letters of reference from such a renowned culinary institute, I would have expected you to try for an entry position in one of the downtown restaurants."

"I was attracted to the challenge and the opportunity to work on my own." She, of course, can't tell Mrs. Floyd the truth—that the thought of diving into the cutthroat world of haute cuisine makes her nauseated. Not a promising reaction for a would-be professional chef.

"I must tell you that normally I would be looking at more experienced chefs, not someone fresh out of school," Mrs. Floyd says.

"I have a lifetime of experience," Lexie says. "I've been cooking since before I could even reach the counter."

"On the other hand," Mrs. Floyd continues, "all of our recent chefs have had extensive professional experience and yet were not a successful fit. Perhaps experience can be a double-edged sword. Those who are too set in their ways have a difficult time adjusting to the demands of this position."

Lexie homes in on the plurals. Just how many occupants of this position have there been, and how many demands were there? Lexie pictures a multitude of chefs spinning about on a giant merry-go-round, each seated on his multicolored wooden steed, his white chef's jacket flapping in the wind, one hand holding on to the pole and the other securing his white toque to the top of his head. Periodically, the merry-go-round stops and takes on one more rider, while simultaneously disgorging yet another disheveled chef to solid ground.

Mrs. Floyd is still speaking. "As I'm sure you've noticed, it's also very isolated here, and you will be alone much of the time."

"That's not a problem. I like having time to myself," Lexie says, adding silently to herself, *Time to breathe; time to recover.*

Mrs. Floyd clears her throat. "There's one more thing. My

employer has a rather unusual and varied palate; he is devoted to all things gastronomic. I always try and anticipate his needs and his moods, and will convey those to you to the best of my ability. Should you be selected for this position, I will see to it that any written notes or instructions and a copy of the next day's schedule are delivered directly to your room each evening."

"I'm sure once I meet him and get involved in the planning, we can work everything out," Lexie says.

"Oh no, my dear. I'm afraid I haven't made myself clear. You won't be working with Mr. Frederick directly. He doesn't like talking to outsiders. In fact, he rarely leaves the estate, except when he's on one of his culinary safaris in search of new gustatory experiences. Everything you need to know will be communicated to you in the form of a written note, or through me."

Lexie frowns. "But how am I to know if I'm succeeding if I can't see or experience his reactions?"

"That, my dear, is the challenge. . . ."

⤚•⤙

Several floors above, John Frederick ponders the process taking place below his feet. Who will Mrs. Floyd choose this time? Certainly the selectee will be physically strong; carrying cast iron skillets is hard work, and requires a degree of muscular development. Clearly he will come draped in an impressive array of credentials and a long history of extensive service. Perhaps he will be a former head chef, looking forward to a stint in a more bucolic environment; or perhaps a pastry chef looking to expand his range of culinary creativity. And perhaps this time he might even be the one, the one who can at last . . . *last*. John Frederick tries to imagine his first taste of the chef's inaugural offering. Whether ultimately satisfying or not, it will at least be a welcome change.

Chapter 2

The Yellow Room

*M*rs. Floyd shows Lexie to her room. Lexie, who has been holding her breath in both anticipation and anxiety, lets out a slow, smooth release of air and a murmured thank-you.

Lexie stares at the yellow walls, her hair a poppy in a field of sunflowers. The room is spare, but contains everything she will need. It is small, neat, and very Lexie, with the same perfect balance of fullness and compactness. As if to cement her sense of belonging, the yellow is almost the same shade as that of the bedroom in her beloved childhood home. "Hello room," she whispers. The curtains, billowing in the suggestion of a breeze, whisper "hello" in return.

Lexie sits on the bed and lays her hand on the stack of sheets, towels, and pillowcases resting by the headboard. "I want to stay here a long time. I *need* to stay here a long time," she murmurs. The insurance money is gone, transformed into payments for the student loans accumulated while at L'Ecole Gastronomique, the school whose certificate of completion and stellar recommendations so impressed Mrs. Floyd. Once again, Lexie says a prayer of thanks for her mother's foresight—the foresight that has allowed her to reach this day, even if it is not the future they once envisioned.

Her mother . . . Lexie's thoughts drift back to happier days.

A much younger Lexie sits on the stone steps tucked away at the side of the yard of her childhood home. Once they led to a small utility shed, long since torn down. This has become Lexie's space, a place she returns to as often as possible. She looks out at the clear, blue sky, broken only by a lone cloud and the lacy tops of the trees at the back of the yard.

The soft, swishy sound of footsteps muffled by the grass causes her to turn her head.

"Hi Mom," she says, a smile forming on her pale, delicate face. The freckles sprinkled across her nose mirror the small brown stones at her feet.

"Mind if I join you?" her mother asks. Lexie's smile widens even further at her mother's appreciation of the sanctity of these steps and innate understanding that, even though the house belongs to Mrs. Haynes, it is Lexie's treasured spot.

"I love this house," Lexie says to her mother. "I love everything about it. Besides, Poppa is here, in these walls. I can feel him."

"You are so his child. He could always sense the story embedded in ordinary things. He always seemed faintly surprised when I couldn't detect the traces of smells and colors and emotions that you two sensed so easily. Remember how he used to look at the bricks lining the fireplace and say they were patinaed by memory?" Her mother takes a moment to swipe at her eyes with the corner of her scarf. "Even after five years, I can't believe he's gone."

"I can't imagine living anywhere else," Lexie says adamantly.

"I'm going to remind you of those words in a year or two when you're away at school. You'll probably never want to come home."

Lexie surveys the room one more time. "No," she says with a sigh, "this yellow is different from my old room." An image of ashes and ruined timbers threatens to eclipse her memory of that golden hue, but she forcibly pushes aside this intruding memory.

"This is a new yellow for a new room," Lexie declares, and, inhaling the welcoming essence of her new domicile, she begins to unpack.

Chapter 3

John Frederick
Takes a Hike

*J*ohn Frederick slowly rises from his bed and stretches his huge arms upward, the flesh on his arms melting back into his shoulders. He takes three deep inhalations. How good it feels to exercise. Buoyed by this rush of activity, John Frederick makes a momentous decision: today will be a hiking day.

To support this energetic inspiration, John Frederick puts on his custom-made tracksuit—a zippered jacket and loose pull-on pants made of a red, satinlike material that stretches easily with each jouncing step. As he surveys himself in the mirror, he is struck by a sudden desire to put on a white ermine scarf and shout "Ho, ho, ho!" but immediately flushes this counterproductive image from his mind.

Using his special long-handled shoehorn, John Frederick snuggles his feet into his elastic-corded athletic shoes. "Nearly ready," he tells himself. All that is left is to provision himself for the coming ordeal. "Two granola bars, peanut-chocolate trail mix, energy drink. That should be enough," he says, mentally checking off each item as he slips it into his capacious pockets.

Thus amply prepared, John Frederick begins his adventure. The path is gentle beneath his feet, carpeted with greenery and flowers. He feels it yield softly with each step, embracing his foot only to spring back into place as he raises his heel and moves forward toward his ultimate destination. John Frederick breathes in the scents that surround him: pine with a hint of fresh rain. What a lovely day!

As he continues, John Frederick's breath begins to quicken, the intake and expulsion of air becoming more and more forced.

"Almost there," he gasps. His goal is tantalizingly in sight. "I shall succeed."

With these last words, he throws himself into the waiting arms of the wide leather chair that has been placed just inside the doorway at the end of the long hallway that leads to what was once his mother's sitting room. John Frederick looks back at the intricately patterned green floral runner stretching into dark recesses of the wing that houses his personal suite and sighs with satisfaction. "Nothing like a little bracing exercise to clear one's head." And then, "I must remember to tell Mrs. Floyd to stock up on more of that new air freshener."

As he rests from his ordeal, John Frederick looks around the room. Except for the chair in which he is ensconced, it looks much as his mother left it. He can almost imagine her sitting on the brocade divan talking to her friend, Clara. They would, as usual, be chatting about art and theater, the fortunes and misfortunes of their acquaintances, and, as a coda to this symphony of gossip, the challenges of family life. Featured prominently among the latter would be the trials of birthing and raising a son. John Frederick could recite, from memory, Alicia Frederick's favorite speech about the ordeal of his premature birth and its impact upon her carefully proscribed life.

"He came so early, how could I possibly have been prepared? The baby nurse hadn't even arrived. I still remember when the maternity nurse took me up to see him. He looked just like some alien creature in a plastic spaceship. So tiny and red and wrinkled. I never would have recognized John Frederick as my baby."

"You were so very brave, Alicia," Clara would respond.

"Yes, motherhood can be so trying."

And then young John Frederick would retreat to his room, wipe his tears, and console himself with a lovely cup of home-made vanilla pudding.

Though time and distance have for the most part taken the sting out of his mother's words, John Frederick still occasionally wishes that she could have added a phrase or two to that last remark, such as "but it was all worth it," or "but it takes effort to produce a positive outcome." Alas, those phrases exist solely in his mind. However, on those rare occasions when sadness and regret threaten to erupt into his consciousness, John Frederick mitigates his mother's judgment as to his adequacy as a son with reminders of his obvious successes. Never once, he consoles himself, did she have to fault him for being a picky eater; and never once did she ever have to say, "Clean your plate, John Frederick. There are children starving in China."

The light of day is beginning to fade. "Time for the return journey," John Frederick mutters. His breathing is now slow and steady. In preparation, he finishes off a granola bar and swallows some trail mix, then washes it down with a swig of the sweet energy drink. "Mustn't get too depleted or I might not make it back."

Chapter 4

The Plaid Flannel Business Suit

*F*inished with her morning tasks, Lexie slips into her well-worn sweater and descends into the garden. It has been six weeks since she entered the Frederick household and she has yet to get even a glimpse of her employer. She has known since her first interview with Mrs. Floyd that John Frederick is a very private man. That is one of the attractions of this job: she is free to cook and experiment without some head chef radiating disdain and criticism looking over her shoulder. But that she will never get any in-person feedback from Mr. Frederick is another matter entirely.

Lexie has always loved to cook. Her fondest memories revolve around the kitchen, sitting perched on a small wooden stepstool and watching her mother's strong, capable hands chop and dice and mix and whisk. Years ago, Lexie asked her mother why she chose to stay at home instead of carving out a profession. "With those hands you could have been a builder, a sculptor, a surgeon," she told her.

"My dearest daughter," her mother replied, "when I create meals for you and your father, I am all of these."

Lexie sometimes feels as if she were still that same child. She is scarcely much taller than she was then, and still needs a stepstool to reach the highest recesses of the kitchen cupboards. Her hair is still the same fiery red, her eyes the same pale gray. Only now that comforting, maternal voice exists only in her fond remembrance and in the passion for cooking that flows through her like water racing to the sea.

As much as Lexie loves her new position, she has begun to wonder about the mysterious Mr. Frederick. Today, the breakfast order specified only something "simple and filling." By now Lexie knows that this is a euphemism for "cook as if the New York Knicks were coming to dine."

Lexie also knows that all that will come back to her will be a tray filled with empty serving dishes and one single large white china plate. Absent any direct interaction with John Frederick, try as she might, Lexie cannot sense in the plate's blank, shiny surface any clue as to what her employer truly thinks of her culinary offerings, or of Lexie herself, other than that her creations are at least palatable enough to warrant complete consumption.

"Cooking is art, cooking is communication." Another echo of her mother's voice floats through Lexie's mind. Yes, that is what she misses: the communication, the joy of preparing a meal attuned to the desires of another person and then observing the reactions to her offering.

Lexie returns her attention to her immediate surroundings, carefully navigating the uneven stone path that weaves through the garden and surrounding grounds. Her senses are filled with the aroma of spring, salvias, and moist earth.

"Mind if I join you?"

Lexie whirls around. Could this be the mysterious Mr.

Frederick at long last? She watches as the man moves easily down the steps, his well-muscled body covered by a plaid flannel shirt and faded jeans.

"You must be the new cook. I'm Caleb—Caleb Mayfield, John Frederick's business manager," says the no-longer-mystery man, extending his hand.

"Alexandra Haynes—Lexie," she responds. Business manager? Don't business managers wear a suit and tie and wingtip shoes? In her mind's eye, Caleb's shirt morphs into a three-piece flannel suit. Lexie blinks to exorcise the image.

Almost as if responding to her thoughts, Caleb adds, "Normally I work in the city, but every once in a while I like to come down and check out the estate in person. There's nothing like actually walking the grounds and knocking on walls to see how things are really going."

As an inveterate talker to walls, trees, and other objects, this all makes perfect sense to Lexie. "Walls can tell you a lot," she replies. Somehow this sounds stranger when she says it aloud.

Caleb pauses to inhale deeply. "Pardon the cliché, but even though I'm a city boy, being here is definitely a breath of fresh air. Besides, I've always been drawn to this garden; perhaps in another life I was a landscape architect."

"It is beautiful," Lexie says. "I want to spend some more time exploring the garden and the rest of the grounds in the future."

"I hope you have many opportunities. I'd love to show you around sometime, but today I'm booked solid. I've got a meeting with John Frederick and some matters to go over with Mrs. Floyd. These face-to-face meetings can be time-consuming, but like I said, I firmly believe there's something about the personal touch. That's been our family's business philosophy since my grandfather's time."

"What's he like?" Lexie asks after a brief pause.

"My grandfather?" Caleb teases.

"No, John Frederick," she says, blushing a little. "You see, I've never actually met him."

"Well, he's . . ." Caleb's words are interrupted by an urgent ringtone, and a worried expression crosses his face. "Speaking of which . . . Please excuse me, but I've got to go. I hope we can continue this conversation sometime in the future."

"Me too," Lexie whispers at Caleb's back as he strides away.

Chapter 5

Traveling Day

John Frederick sits in front of the window, looking at the overcast sky. He usually prefers to experience his weather by proxy, relying on the weather channel or the informational box in the top corner of his computer screen, but today is different. It is a traveling day.

"It's been too long since I went on a culinary safari," he says to the John Frederick reflected in the tinted window glass. "I hope we will be able to fly out."

As John Frederick continues to stare, he notices one lighter, puffier cloud visible through a break in the gray sky. It reminds him of the bowl of clotted cream he had when he journeyed to Great Britain a number of years ago for the quintessential afternoon tea. Clotted cream, gooseberry jam, fresh-baked scones flecked with tiny currants, and those crustless sandwiches cut into triangles and filled with cucumber, watercress, and assorted other delicacies. "Those Brits sure know how to set a table," he muses. "Perhaps I'll have the new chef prepare tea for me. I wonder if you can get Branston Pickle in the United States."

Today's destination does not involve a trip over the pond, but rather a shorter jaunt to San Antonio. John Frederick hums "The Yellow Rose of Texas" as he begins to select his wardrobe for the trip. He ponders a Western theme, but decides that the cowboy hat and fringed leather vest seem a bit excessive. Besides, the Stetson will make an unflattering dent in his thick brown hair should he choose to take it off later. A silver and turquoise bolo tie is similarly rejected. John Frederick ultimately opts for comfort and lays out several loose cotton shirts and generously elasticized pants. The rejected clothes form a pile of color on the side of the bed.

As he begins to pack, he runs his finger over the brown leather binding of his suitcase, its smooth surface marred by years of use, first as the valise of choice for John Frederick, Sr., and now for John Frederick. Even though he does not travel often, preferring his own surroundings, his own company, and the assurance of ample supplies of gustatory necessities, John Frederick nonetheless likes to be prepared. His suitcase, therefore, is stuffed with both clothing and caloric necessities. In a similar vein, he knows his private plane will be fueled and fully stocked with readily available snacks, lest he be overcome with hunger while en route.

John Frederick smiles in anticipation of this newest safari. San Antonio, a lovely town and reportedly home to the best barbecue in Texas, awaits. And oh yes, isn't it also known for the Alamo?

⁂

The sun has begun to set when, sated and content, John Frederick pushes his body back from the table, his hands blood red and sticky with barbecue sauce.

"Please tell Jorge that this brisket is superb," he calls to the waiter, who is lingering unobtrusively by the door to the empty banquet room. "And the ribs—nirvana." He wipes his hand on a red-checked cloth napkin. "And tell Jorge that perhaps I will have that pecan pie now."

John Frederick smiles as the man brings him the pie-filled plate. He digs in his fork and brings it to his mouth. Ah, the crunchiness of the nuts, the smooth, sweet caress of the filling, and the soft, buttery flakiness of the crust.

John Frederick listens briefly to the muffled sounds of voices and clinking plates coming from the public dining room, and wonders briefly what it would be like if he were to dine with someone else.

The bell rings and another lunch period at Mt. Pearson Middle School bursts into exuberant existence. Children and proto-teens spill out into the yard, some with lunch boxes and paper sacks, others with bills and jingling change to buy macaroni supreme, blue hot dogs in cardboard buns, and, most important of all, cream-filled, soft-textured Twinkies from the waiting vending machine.

John Frederick is sitting at his usual table on the far side of the lunch yard. His bulk takes up one side of the table; the other side remains empty as usual. His stomach pushes against the table top, but the space is unexpandable, the bench and table set in concrete.

John Frederick opens his lunch box, or rather his lunch attaché. It is filled with hardboiled eggs, and two carefully constructed sandwiches on whole wheat bread: one of tuna salad spiced with sweet pickles, and one with cream cheese and raisins. A silver Thermos flask nests in a special pocket on the side. John Frederick knows that inside, dangling from a string, is one large, fat sausage, kept warm by the steaming soup.

"I am this sausage," he thinks, "large, stuffed, and enshrined in an insulated casing." He is rather pleased with this metaphor, voracious reader that he is. Taking out the Thermos, he sets it upright on the table's scarred wooden surface and unscrews the cap that also turns into a cup. He tugs on the string, pulls out the sausage, and takes his first bite. His teeth clang together with a resounding click that pushes away from his consciousness any unkind remarks borne on the wind from the other side of the yard.

His musings thus answered by this spew of childhood memories, John Frederick shakes his head. "No," he murmurs, "I will not let those memories spoil this perfect day."

Safe and alone, he finishes his meal.

Chapter 6

Lexie's Bravery

*J*ohn Frederick has left the house for the day. Even without the written note from Mrs. Floyd, delivered to Lexie's room last evening as part of the daily routine, Lexie would have been aware of that fact. The house is filled with his absence.

Lexie enters the kitchen and begins heating water for her morning tea. No electric teakettles in this kitchen, only the direct caress of flame to metal and the dance of liquid molecules within the round belly of the kettle. Lexie can always tell when the water has reached the right temperature by the sound of the agitated molecules. A soft dance means the temperature is perfect for white tea, a more vigorous line dance signals oolong readiness, and a tarantella, black-tea perfection.

"What shall I do today?" she muses as she sips her steaming cup of Earl Grey. "Walk in the gardens, go into town, or maybe even read an entire book?"

Instead, to her surprise, Lexie finds herself walking slowly up the staircase that leads to John Frederick's private suite. The wooden banister is worn smooth and there is a faint indentation in the center of each step. Did John Frederick climb these stairs once upon a time? Lexie knows he now usually takes the private elevator.

Surely the door will be locked. The reclusive John Frederick will have seen to that. Lexie takes a deep breath and does the bravest thing she has ever done.

She turns the knob and, finding it unlocked, opens the door.

Astonished, Lexie looks around the room. It is large, dimly lit, and dominated by a large bed mounded with comforters. The room smells slightly musty but is overlaid with complex scents. She inhales the smell of cedar and sadness, the deep purple odor of loneliness and longing—with a hint of poetry—and then yes, a smell so powerful that when it enters her nostrils, it fills her entire body and blots out every other olfactory stimulus: the bright, shining odor of John Frederick's joy in consuming her cooking.

Lexie feels the tears cascading down her cheeks. Her knees weaken, and she collapses into the waiting caress of the soft, handwoven rug that adorns the floor.

⌐•⌐

John Frederick enters his room. He is both exhilarated and exhausted after his culinary safari to Texas. His bed looks soft and inviting, and he is tempted to simply fall upon the covers and surrender, abandoning all preparatory ritual. But as he moves toward the bed, he notices a pile of clothes on the floor. Did he fling them there? He always tries on and discards multiple outfits when he prepares to enter the outside world, yet he cannot remember actually throwing the rejects onto the floor.

He moves closer, still staring at the multicolored heap on the floor, and sees a white arm—almost fluorescent in the darkness—and a tumbled mass of red hair, deepened to auburn in the dimness. It reminds him of nothing so much as a giant piece of iced gingerbread smashed against the carpet. He is stunned into silence. Suddenly the gingerbread opens its eyes and screams. John Frederick feels himself falling backward onto the bed. Displaced by his weight, the duvet and covers rise above him like waves.

John Frederick struggles to push himself upright. He hears the rustling of fabric but can't tell if it comes from his own efforts or from the floor. Confusion, rage, betrayal, and humiliation struggle for control of his tongue. The words that emerge are very loud but strangely devoid of affect. "Get out!" he says, and the piece of gingerbread, now standing, turns and disappears out into the awaiting corridor.

John Frederick closes his eyes and replays the scene over and over again, each replay colored by another emotion. The intruder has violated the only "inviolate" rule of the house. He has deduced that the invader must be the new chef, since no one else would dare to commit such a crime, and the size and color of the fleeing confection matched the general description Mrs. Floyd gave him of the new hire. But even newness does not excuse such egregious behavior, and John Frederick knows he should summon Mrs. Floyd at once and have her dismiss the offender from his household. He reaches for the call button, but feels the wave of his earlier fatigue, reenergized by the stew of his emotions, sweep over him. His eyelids close as he drops once again to the bed. *I'll take care of it tomorrow*, he thinks as he slips into peaceful unconsciousness.

◆•◆

Lexie slams the door to her room and begins pacing back and forth with short, quick strides. "How can I have been so stupid?" she asks herself over and over again. "How can I have screwed up so badly?" She knows that at any second Mrs. Floyd will be at the door, termination papers in hand.

Lexie relives the fiasco in vivid detail—the opening of her eyes, the huge bulk looming before her, filling every inch of her vision. For one horrible moment, she had thought that there couldn't be room in the surrounding space for anything else, and she might be pushed out of existence by that mountain of flesh. She remembers the terror rising up through her body and then pushing outward into a scream. She remembers the force of it pulling her upright while at the same time it pushed John Frederick back onto his bed.

But then she remembers an earlier moment: the shower of emotions she felt just before she sank, unconscious, into the carpet. She senses once again John Frederick's pleasure and joy in consuming her gifts. He has taken her offerings with such gusto and enjoyment that the echoes of his emotions have filled the room just as her food has filled his body. This, too, was John Frederick.

Lexie pauses and shakes her head. Once again she sees his giant frame—the sheer bulk of him, his immensity of flesh— but this time her head is filled with wonderment. All this flesh is partially her creation. *Her* hands, *her* creativity, have produced the offerings that have nourished and expanded this living, breathing work of art. Her cooking has had meaning all along.

The adrenaline drains from her body and her fingers uncurl from their clenched position. Lexie wishes she could touch that flesh, feel its malleable softness. She wants to caress the surface where the air stops and John Frederick begins. But now it is too late.

Spent, Lexie slides onto the overstuffed chair in the corner. *I'll just lie here and wait for the inevitable.* Surely, Mrs. Floyd will knock on the door soon. *Yes, I've truly blown it,* Lexie thinks as she drifts into a restless sleep.

Chapter 7

Aftermath

L exie opens her eyes. She is still awkwardly sprawled in the chair, one leg bent beneath her. She stretches out her legs and arms, feeling the stiffness in her neck and lower back. Her foot tingles in protest.

Lexie slips into her favorite jeans and soft T-shirt. Although these are her comfort clothes, today they bring no comfort, and she wraps her sadness around her like a cloak. Surprisingly, she has received no formal notice, but Lexie knows that this will be her last day at Frederick House.

She sees her white chef's jacket hanging on its familiar peg by the doorway. She touches its starched finish, regretfully acknowledging that there is no need for it today. Then she shakes her head. *This may be my last day*, she thinks, *but I might as well make my final exit with dignity.* With reawakened resolve, Lexie puts on her white armor and heads towards the kitchen.

John Frederick is walking down the stairs. He so seldom uses this means of egress that the treads feel unfamiliar beneath his feet. Normally he leaves all household matters, the hirings and firings of staff, to Mrs. Floyd. But today he feels he must make an exception. He has been personally violated and so the retaliation must also be personally administered. Despite the unpleasant task that awaits him, he rather enjoys the challenge of the stairs—the act of balancing his huge body, his weight shifting from one side to the other, as he descends.

Perhaps in the future he will add this trek as an alternative route for his hiking regimen. Already he can see himself dressed as a Swiss mountaineer, staff in hand, wearing custom-made lederhosen and colorfully embossed suspenders. This reverie carries John Frederick to the bottom of the stairway, where he stops to regain his focus and wait for his breath to resume a semblance of normal rhythm.

Recovered at last, John Frederick stands in the kitchen doorway surveying the scene before him. A small young woman is working at the counter, her delicate hands moving back and forth between a series of small bowls filled with contents of varying hues and shapes. It is Alexandra Haynes, yesterday's invader of his lair. John Frederick decides that although she is no longer smashed pastry, her hair is indeed the color of gingerbread—or more accurately, carrot cake, since daylight has rendered her hair a somewhat lighter hue.

The woman shows no sign of awareness that she is being observed. Apparently even the sounds and echoes heralding John Frederick's passage have failed to register. In spite of himself, John Frederick is impressed by the woman's power of concentration. It is such a shame that she has proved herself so unworthy of his trust.

John Frederick lowers himself onto a sturdy wooden chair.

It creaks in protest but accepts the burden. This time the sound of his arrival has a definite effect on the new chef: she whirls around, and her hand crushes the eggshell she has just started to crack. The shell splits into a network of fissures and its contents slither onto the floor.

"I am so sorry," the woman cries as she grabs a towel and drops to her knees. The room is momentarily silent as she attempts to corral the gelatinous mess glittering against the immaculate ceramic tiles. John Frederick watches as, successful at last, she rises, squares her shoulders and begins to speak.

"I know that I've done something horrible, unforgivable," she says. "But please give me a chance to explain."

For a moment, John Frederick is surprised by this level of contrition over the loss of an egg; then he realizes she is referring to yesterday's transgression. His anger returns.

"You have to understand. I can't just cook in a vacuum. I have to cook *for* someone. I thought it would be okay, that I could handle it, but I couldn't. I just had to know you."

John Frederick looks directly into her eyes. They remind him of blueberry sorbet mixed with cream. The words "You're dismissed" form in his head, but when they emerge from his mouth, they have morphed into an unexpected phrase. "Well, Ms. Haynes, perhaps just this once, I forgive you."

Chapter 8

Time Passes— Notes Part I

FROM THE DESK OF JOHN FREDERICK

Dear Ms. Haynes,

The pot roast was excellent.

John Frederick

FROM THE DESK OF JOHN FREDERICK

Dear Ms. Haynes,

I so enjoyed your coq au vin.

Thank you,

John Frederick

FROM THE DESK OF JOHN FREDERICK

Dear Ms. Haynes,

The spices you added to the poached salmon made such a difference.

It was a pleasure eating it.

Thank you,

John Frederick

FROM THE DESK OF JOHN FREDERICK

Dear Lexie,

The cassoulet was wonderful. It was such a perfect dish for a cold, blustery day. How did you know that it was exactly what I needed?

You are a treasure,

John Frederick

Chapter 9

Ribbit

*E*ach day Lexie cooks with renewed vigor. Each day she is rewarded by John Frederick's handwritten note, detailing his thoughts and reactions. *This must be what Momma meant when she talked about preparing meals for Poppa and me, and how both the artistry and our response filled and fulfilled her,* Lexie muses as she reaches for the latest note. *Perhaps one day John Frederick will even come back again into the kitchen so I can experience his enjoyment in person.*

Lexie opens her eyes, luxuriating in the promise of a beautiful and unencumbered morning. Instead of breakfast and lunch, John Frederick has asked that she prepare an old-fashioned brunch, to be served later than his usual morning repast. Lexie smiles at the thought of this distinction, since John Frederick's breakfast often runs right into his lunch, making this latest request more a matter of semantics and timing than a significant change.

With several hours now free, Lexie decides to spend the time exploring the garden. It is chilly outside, so she layers herself in jeans and a turtleneck, a warm sweater and a windbreaker. Just to be on the safe side, she tucks her hair under her knit ski cap. Surveying herself in the mirror, Lexie notes that a strand of hair has already escaped, adding a flash of orange-red to the blue, green and yellow stripes of her colorful headgear. She also notes that she looks like a bundled up twelve-year-old about to be taken on an outing to the park. Imbued with this spirit, Lexie finds herself skipping down the stairs to the garden.

Lexie looks across the colorful panorama of green and gold and shadow. It is lovely to have the grounds all to herself on such a sparkling day. Still, she cannot help but remember that the last time she spent any time in this venue was the day she met handsome Caleb Mayfield.

Then, almost as if she has conjured him into being by her memories, a figure passes into her field of vision. No, it can't be Caleb; there was nothing on the day's schedule about a business meeting with him, nor has there been any mention of cooking for two (that is, besides the fact that the portions she cooks for John Frederick are so large they could easily be for two, or even more).

Yet somehow it is indeed Caleb Mayfield. He looks, she notices, like an L.L.Bean catalogue model, and for the first time she wishes she had chosen something slightly more flattering for her morning outing. Lexie starts to wave—then, overcome by a rush of shyness, lowers her hand. He is altogether too handsome.

"Stop it," she admonishes herself in a whisper. "I don't have room for childish crushes. I'm an adult." Then, louder, she calls out, "Hello, Mr. Mayfield." The use of the more formal greeting steadies her voice.

"Good to see you, Lexie, and, please, call me Caleb." He smiles as he approaches her.

"I didn't realize you were scheduled to come down to Frederick House today . . . Caleb."

"It's an unplanned visit. They're doing some restoration work on one of the outbuildings, and the architect and the contractor are at each other's throats. I thought I'd better come out in person to straighten things out before they start lobbing bricks at each other, or worse."

"And did you succeed?"

"I think I've brokered a peace for now, so I'm taking advantage of the ceasefire by getting in a morning walk."

Lexie decides to throw caution to the wind. After all, if she was brave enough to enter John Frederick's inner sanctum, she should be brave enough to take Caleb up on his earlier offer to act as tour guide.

"Do you think you might have time to show me around a little?"

"It would be my pleasure. My only condition is that we stay far way from the battlefield." Caleb pauses. "Wait, I've got an idea. I hope you're up for some exercise?"

"No problem, although I do have to get back in time to prepare John Frederick's brunch."

"Then follow me. I know a place with an amazing view. And it's on the opposite side of the grounds from the restoration work."

He sets off, and Lexie falls into step beside him.

"So how are things going?" Caleb asks as they begin their journey. "Is everything working out?"

"Oh yes. I love it here. And I finally got to meet John Frederick."

"And . . ."

"Well, he's different than I expected, but I think he's pleased with my performance so far."

"You must be very good at your job."

As they continue, Lexie notices that the garden is becoming noticeably less manicured and more densely covered with trees. Off to her right she catches a glimpse of a tall tree whose graceful limbs curve back towards the ground. Lexie senses there is something special about this tree and makes a mental note to return as soon as possible.

Caleb is apparently caught up in his own ruminations; he is silent except for the sound of his breathing and the scuffing of his thick-soled shoes against the gravel.

Soon, the garden abandons any pretense of civilized obedience and gives way to natural woodland.

"We're getting close," Caleb says, the sound of his voice gliding through the silence. "Be careful on this next stretch. It can be a bit slippery."

Indeed, the gradually sloping path now begins to wind up a rock-strewn hill.

"I'll be fine," Lexie says. She was once a dancer, after all—or at least a would-be dancer. Of course, that was many years ago, when she was a child. Still, she negotiates the climb with only a slight twinge of protest from her calves. She joins Caleb at the top of the rise feeling triumphant.

"It's beautiful," she says, looking out across the tree-covered vale spread out before them. "It's like another world."

Caleb gestures toward a fallen log. "Sit down for a moment so you can take it all in. This is one of my favorite places. I remember how excited I was as a boy when I first found this spot."

"You grew up here?"

"No, of course not. But my father was John Frederick Senior's advisor, so I sometimes came with him and spent the time exploring while they conducted business."

"I wish I could spend more time exploring too, but I've got to get back." Lexie rises from the log, promptly steps on a loose rock, and finds herself descending the hill in a much faster manner than she anticipated.

"Whoa, girl," Caleb says, helping her up. "I told you, this part can be slippery. Are you okay?"

Lexie, blushing in embarrassment, flexes her foot. "My ankle is a little sore but nothing serious. I'm sure walking will loosen it up."

"Well, just to be safe, why don't you hang on to my arm on the way back. Sometimes it's just when you think everything is all right that you take a tumble."

Lexie grips Caleb's arm, and with his firm support she manages the trek back to Frederick House without further incident.

"I'll just make sure you make it up the steps okay," Caleb says as they reach the rear entryway.

"I think my foot's recovered, but thank you for your offer," Lexie says. "Why don't you let me show my appreciation by whipping up some breakfast for you while I start my prep work on John Frederick's meal? I could do a nice frittata with Gruyère cheese and *fines herbes.*"

"That's really nice of you, but I had a protein shake on the ride over and I don't usually eat during the day," Caleb says. "I'm afraid I'm one of those people who view food as fuel rather than art."

"What?" Lexie asks in disbelief. Food as nothing more than fuel? What does that make her, a gas station attendant? Alas, her Prince Charming begins to turn into a frog before her very eyes. In fact, Lexie notices, there does seem to be a hint of green next to his temples. She blinks and the image disappears, although there is still the slightest whiff of lily ponds and damp mud.

"I'm so sorry," Caleb says. "I can see where that might have sounded insulting. It's not that I don't appreciate the effort that goes into creating a good meal, but I'm just not a foodie. I know that's a shameful confession from a supposed city sophisticate like me. I hope you'll keep my secret."

Sadly, Lexie nods her head, and watches as Caleb reaches into his pocket and pulls out a business card.

"I stashed a few of these away in case I needed them this morning. This one's for you. You never know when you might need a friend in the city, or a guide to Chez Frederick."

Lexie reaches up and fingers the embossed white card. Well, he is a rather kind frog, and even amphibian friendship might not be such a bad thing, given the lack of other candidates. Although Mrs. Floyd greets Lexie cordially each day and is solicitous about her welfare, it is clear to Lexie that the older woman wishes to maintain a professional distance. As for the daily staff, they come and go without remark, leaving no trace save the smell of furniture polish and air freshener. Caleb at least talks to her. Besides, having an expert on John Frederick and Frederick House might come in handy someday. Lexie looks up and smiles, suppressing an urge to respond with a resounding, "Ribbit."

"Thank you, Caleb. And thank you for the walk."

⌐•⌐

Later that evening, filled with the delicious tiredness of a day well spent, Lexie opens the door to her yellow room.

I'm going to treat myself to a nice long bubble bath, she decides. Moments later she glides into the hot, fragrant water, sinking down until her head is partially submerged. The bubbles tickle her nose, and she feels her muscles unkink.

Afterwards, when she climbs out of the tub, her legs feel so soft and boneless that she nearly loses her footing. She doesn't even bother with a nightgown but slips in between the covers, her skin still slightly damp.

The day has rewound and it is morning again, but this time the sun has just begun to rise, and Lexie and Caleb, enveloped in pink and gold, are standing side by side gazing at the brilliantly colored almost-morning sky. Caleb draws her towards him and Lexie, eyes now closed, glides easily into his arms. She is surprised at how large his body feels as she leans against him. He bends down and touches her lips with his. They are much fuller, more sensuous, than she had imagined, so wonderfully hard and soft. Her eyes still closed, Lexie reaches up to touch his cheek. It is so round and plump, so tantalizing to her touch. She feels herself beginning to tumble, vibrating with an energy that begins in her core and—

The alarm jerks Lexie awake. For one brief moment she lies suspended between waking and sleeping. Her pre–alarm clock internal wakeup mechanism has failed her, and this unexpected interruption wipes the details of her dream from her mind. All that is left is a residual feeling of joy and anticipation.

Chapter 10

John Frederick and the Cancelled Breakfast

*T*he alarm sounds. John Frederick throws off the covers, thrashing into semiwakefulness. He wipes his eyes, gummed with unslept hours, and reaches towards the sound coming from the oh-so-distant bedside table.

And then he remembers. Lexie will be making breakfast. It doesn't matter that she has cooked breakfast every day for the past few months. Last night, he decided that this would be the first morning he would join her to eat. But that was last night, and now is now. He again stretches toward the nightstand, this time successfully hitting the button that silences the clock.

There is no sound in the bedroom except for John Frederick's slight wheeze. It is once again the perfect cocoon. And yet his eyes are still open, and he is beginning to feel surprisingly alert. He feels the corners of his mouth move ever so slightly.

John Frederick is smiling. He continues to smile until his gaze reaches the window—where, to further reduce any chance of oversleeping, the blackout curtains he usually keeps drawn have been deliberately kept open. Even from his supine position he can see his rolling green lawn, the vibrant colors of the garden, and something foreign and unexpected: two shapes walking side by side.

As he focuses on this sight, the shapes become recognizable as Caleb Mayfield and someone with multicolored hair. John Frederick has seen Caleb in the garden many times, but his companion is a mystery—until, that is, the couple's continued progress toward the house reveals the second person to be none other than a knit-capped Lexie. And if this were not unsettling enough, what John Frederick assumed until now was empty space between them is clearly occupied by Caleb and Lexie's intertwined arms. Smiles and resolve swept aside, John Frederick stumbles from his bed, angrily pulls the curtains back across the windows, and reduces the room to blessed darkness. The offending view now blocked from his sight if not from his mind, he sinks slowly into bed, rolls onto his side, and fitfully falls asleep.

John Frederick is awake. The room is dark, the curtains drawn, and only a tiny line of silver between the two drapery panels tell him that it is day rather than night. Lying in the darkness, John Frederick feels disconnected, untethered, yet at the same time so heavy that his body might simply crash through the bed, the floorboards, and the rooms below. John Frederick does not recognize these feelings, knowing only that they are connected somehow to the giant hole that has opened up in his chest and his belly.

He reaches over to his bedside table and fingers open the

drawer, which slides noiselessly until the catch mechanism stops its progress. John Frederick wishes he had a catch mechanism on his life. He inserts two more fingers and pulls at the edge of a plastic-wrapped bundle. He doesn't even look at its contents as he tears it apart with his teeth and lets part of the contents spill into his mouth. He realizes it is a bag of chocolate-covered pretzels, and the sweet saltiness is like a balm to his soul.

The masticated pretzels have barely passed his gullet when he takes the bag from his mouth and pulls out another handful. Adrift as he his, he still feels the need to maintain a modicum of dignity, and having gotten the first hit, prefers to use his hands now, as a person of civilized upbringing would. Besides, using his hands to transfer food from a container to his mouth scarcely slows down the process.

John Frederick reaches for a second bag. This time his treasure hunt produces a bag of Oreos. Usually he would separate each cookie and, in the time-honored tradition of champion Oreo eaters, lick the cloying white inner filling clean before popping the dark, perforated circles into his mouth. Today, he inserts the entire cookie, followed immediately by one of its companions, and then another, and another.

John Frederick can feel equilibrium returning. The floating feeling and heaviness meet and he is now merely lying slightly upright in his bed. His sensation of emptiness has also receded, although somewhere in his consciousness he knows that it is still there. For the moment, however, he feels only a wonderful numbness, perhaps even a twinge of endorphin high.

Thus fortified, John Frederick rises slowly from his bed and heads to the bathroom to answer a call of nature that even his desire for continued lethargy cannot erase. Returning from the marble-tiled bathroom, he is motivated enough to open the heavy curtains.

As he gazes at the view, another emotion pushes itself into the space so newly paved over with Oreos and pretzels. The garden, once an innocent expanse of flora and occasional fauna, is now almost unbearably haunted by memory. A red wave of jealousy-fueled rage rises up through John Frederick's body.

"I will tear out the garden," he mutters through clenched teeth. He can see the machinery plowing through the grass and blossoms, ripping out the growth by its roots, the greens and reds and yellows and pinks consumed by the dark brown earth. He can almost smell the loamy odor of this planned desecration. Perhaps he could put in a rock garden—or, even better, cover it with concrete.

John Frederick smiles tightly and lumbers back to his bedside. He grabs a chocolate cupcake from the drawer, crams it into his mouth, and then, once again calm, levers himself back into bed. Perhaps, he muses, rather than physically destroying the garden—which is, after all, an integral part of Frederick House—he can simply ensure that it will never again be desecrated by the presence of Caleb Mayfield. Regretfully, Caleb is too valuable an advisor to dismiss completely—but there is no reason why he cannot forever be banned from putting foot to garden path. But as for Lexie . . . John Frederick's mind cannot even go there.

Chapter 11

The Silence

*L*exie can tell that something is terribly wrong. She has had no communication from John Frederick for three days—no notes of appreciation or even of criticism. She knows that he is in residence, so physical absence cannot explain this lapse. She is surprised at how stricken she feels. Up until this inexplicable recent lapse in correspondence, Lexie had thought John Frederick might even be contemplating a trek downstairs for breakfast. This soufflé of hope has now collapsed.

She sits at the kitchen table, carefully avoiding the space where John Frederick sat that fateful day he bestowed upon her his forgiveness for her trespassing into his inner sanctum. This is, and will forever be in her mind, a place belonging uniquely to one person, not to be invaded without invitation. *Have I done something wrong?* she demands of herself. What has happened to the John Frederick of that last note, the John Frederick who praised her cooking and came closer to her with each missive? Where, in fact, is *any* John Frederick? Perhaps he is ill or in despair. Mrs. Floyd has not mentioned anything about him being sick, but this fact brings Lexie no comfort. In her mind's eye, Lexie can see his body lying on the floor, a huge pale lump, alone and abandoned. It is more than she can stand.

For the second time, now drawn by worry instead of curiosity, Lexie finds herself ascending the stairs to John Frederick's suite. It requires such an effort, as if she herself has somehow taken on her employer's bulk. Each creak of the wood says, "Don't do this, be silent," but she ignores the admonition and continues upward.

With a trembling hand, she knocks on the door and softly calls his name. She takes a step backward and prepares to wait, knowing that even if John Frederick is in good health, it will take him a few minutes to traverse his room. Instead, the door swings open at once, almost as if he were anticipating her arrival.

"John Frederick!" she exclaims in a startled voice.

"Who else would you expect? Caleb Mayfield, perhaps?"

"Caleb! What does he have to do with anything?" Lexie studies John Frederick's face. Perhaps he is indeed ill and is suffering from some fever-induced mental instability.

"Don't play Ms. Innocence with me. I'm surprised you even have time to cook in between dalliances."

Lexie's confusion over John Frederick's remarks is growing. "But I've only seen Caleb Mayfield twice in my life. He was kind enough to show me around the estate a few days ago, but that's it. And he certainly hasn't interfered in any way with my duties as a chef."

As she says these words, Lexie realizes that they are truer than she realized until this moment. It is not Caleb but something else that has begun to fill her heart. This realization, however, does little to erase her sense of indignation. Lexie can feel the heat exploding from her cheeks and forehead, and then, as if summoned to put out the fire, the first trickle of tears. She cries out, "There isn't really room for anyone in my life anyway. I put all my heart and soul into every dish I create for you."

Overwhelmed, Lexie closes her eyes and takes several slow breaths. She conjures up her memory of the first time she entered John Frederick's room, when the bright shining odor of his joy in consuming her cooking flooded her. Now, that scent is almost undetectable, buried beneath layers of anger and accusation. Lexie turns all her focus on that delicate remnant, willing it to expand.

After a few moments she opens her eyes. Whether due to the cooling-off period provided by her silence, her declaration of innocence, or a certain subtle fragrance beginning to waft about the room, Lexie can see John Frederick's face softening.

"Perhaps I've been a bit hasty in my judgments," he offers.

Lexie nods encouragingly.

"Yes," John Frederick says, "I have definitely been too quick to jump to conclusions."

Lexie nods again. There is another pause.

"I, uh . . ." John Frederick seems to be struggling to find the right words. "I can see that you are a wonderful chef, and your devotion to your craft is exceptional. I am sorry for my behavior."

And in a flash, Lexie realizes that in *this* encounter, it is John Frederick who is asking for forgiveness. She looks up with a smile.

"Well, Mr. Frederick, perhaps just this once, I forgive you."

Chapter 12

Darkness, Light, and Marjoram

*J*ohn Frederick watches as Lexie puts the kettle on the front burner of the large industrial cooktop. John Frederick still cannot quite believe that he is: a) actually physically sitting in the kitchen, and b) anticipating with pleasure, as well as trepidation, the sharing of the space with another, also physically present human being.

"What type of tea would you prefer today?" Lexie asks. "The water is just reaching the right temperature for oolong."

"Yes, I think oolong would be quite nice. Perhaps the Auspicious Ayame Wulong."

Lexie nods. For the next few moments the only sound in the room is the small clink of a spoon inserted into a tea tin, the tiny rustling whisper as the tea leaves are gently shaken into the strainer, and the muted gurgling of water as it is transferred from kettle to teapot. Precisely three minutes later, John Frederick notes approvingly, the tea is poured into a china cup and presented to him.

John Frederick takes a sip, smiles, and gestures toward the seat opposite his own. "Please, won't you join me?"

Judging from her expression, the fact that he has actually said these words out loud is as much a surprise to his red-haired chef as it is to John Frederick.

"And how are you finding things here at Frederick House?" he asks as Lexie takes her seat. "I realize it's not everyone's, er, cup of tea." He smiles inwardly at this choice of phrase. "Several of my employees have found the relative isolation too stressful. I personally find it quite comfortable, but I've been on my own here—except, of course for Mrs. Floyd and the staff—ever since my parents died."

"Were you very young?" Lexie asks. "It can't have been easy for you."

"Not so young. I was sixteen at the time. I was sitting in my room reading a book about astronomy and thinking how much I would like to go into outer space, if only they would start making more commodious space capsules. There was a knock on the door and in walked Harrison Mayfield, my father's attorney and business manager. I don't think I would have been more surprised if it had been a space alien. You see, I'd never seen Mr. Mayfield except when accompanied by my father, and, of course, never in my private rooms."

A stray thought intrudes. *Well, there was that time Mr. Mayfield brought in his son, thinking the two of us might be friends. How they thought I would have anything in common with that stringy, awkward geek, I'll never know. Thank heavens Caleb mellowed over time.*

"I knew something was wrong because Mr. Mayfield looked so strange," John Frederick continues. "No suit, no tie, just a sweater and casual pants, and he had this strained expression on his face. It's funny, even though it's been twenty years, I can remember every word he said: 'John Frederick, please excuse this intrusion, but I have something I felt must be told to you in person. This is going to be a shock, but you must be strong.' Then he moved towards me and put his hand on my shoulder, which was also very strange. Then he said, 'There's been a terrible accident. Your parents' plane went down early this morning. There are no survivors. John Frederick, your parents are gone.'"

"Poor John Frederick," Lexie says softly. "My parents are gone, too, so I can imagine how you must have felt. I was only twelve when my father died, but my mother has been gone less than a year. I still miss her so much. Do you miss your parents?"

John Frederick realizes he doesn't know how to answer Lexie's question. Does he miss them? *I must have missed them at the time,* he thinks. *They were my parents, and they loved me, and they did everything they could to ensure that I would be raised in the proper way. I knew they were always there—well, maybe* there *more often than* here, *but still contactable.* The word "reachable" just doesn't seem to fit.

"It was such a chaotic time," he says out loud. "All those arrangements and papers and that constant stream of strangers coming in and out to make condolence calls. The only good thing was that they did bring food."

John Frederick pauses while he conjures up the image of his younger self, sitting in his dark bedroom, consuming slice after slice of chocolate cake. He does not share this vision with Lexie, but instead returns to her original question.

"But did I miss them? I kept waiting to cry, for all those paroxysms of tears like I'd read about, but even though I was truly sad, they never came. I remember thinking, *Perhaps the tear ducts are compressed in very large people.*"

John Frederick watches Lexie's face with concern. Has he been talking too much? Has he overstepped his bounds? This has certainly been an unexpected conversation. John Frederick is, therefore, quite relieved when she smiles in what seems like reassuring sympathy. Perhaps he should allow Lexie time to comment. Or, even more daring, inquire about her own experience. He takes another large swallow of tea.

"And how was it for you?" he asks, blushing slightly as he realizes that in all the novels he has read, this question is asked under very different circumstances.

Thankfully Lexie responds to the single, not double, entendre.

"I was in my dorm room at culinary school when I got the call. I picked up the phone and everything just disintegrated. I know you said you remember every word, but all I can remember are bits and pieces: 'Are you Alexandra Haynes? . . . I'm afraid I have some bad news . . . fire . . . house . . . mother . . .'" She swallows. "And then all these thoughts came rushing in. Those I can remember *too* clearly. I called out, 'Mother, help me, I'm an orphan!' even though I knew it made no sense. It felt like I had no place, no identity, nowhere to stand. I kept thinking, *I have to go home. She can't be dead. Wait, there is no home. No, that isn't possible. There must be something left. It's all a mistake, a big mistake.*

John Frederick sits frozen, unsure of what to say.

"And then the next thing I knew I was in my car driving home," Lexie says.

"And was there anything left?"

"Nothing. Just charred wood, soot, and twisted metal pipes. I couldn't feel any trace of my parents at all."

John Frederick feels a chill run down his neck. He can picture her standing there, completely, totally alone, her red hair a mocking echo of the now-extinguished flames that had wrought such destruction. He can almost smell the burnt black smell.

"And everything was infused with that awful dark scent of

loss," Lexie continues. "I couldn't smell anything else for a long time."

"My dear Lexie, how did you go on?"

"I didn't—at least, not at first. I rented a room and just curled up in that darkness, until one day I found myself standing in the market in front of the spice section. And I could smell them all! Lemon pepper, cinnamon, turmeric, and marjoram. I just kept putting jars and ingredients in my cart. By the time I got back home I had two bags of groceries and a very heavy cast-iron skillet.

"And as I chopped and stirred and sautéed, I could almost feel my mother standing behind me. I wanted to say to her, 'Momma, see, I'm letting the onions cook a long, long time so the dish won't be spoiled by undercooked onions.' And that's how I began cooking again."

"I'm so glad you did," said John Frederick, unconsciously patting his stomach. "Frederick House would be so much blander without you."

John Frederick notices that Lexie's eyes have acquired a distinct sheen. *Could it be because of those remembered onions?* he wonders. Yet as he watches her eyes start to blur, something very odd begins to happen inside his own body.

"Got to go. Business," John Frederick mumbles as he feels the very unexpected sensation of twenty years of unexpressed tears begin to flow down his pillowy cheeks and onto the white napkin tucked beneath his chins. In an effort to outrace the coming inundation, he pushes himself out of his chair and lumbers out the door.

Chapter 13

Oolonging

*J*ohn Frederick sits in the welcome isolation of his room, recuperating from his frenzied exodus from the kitchen. The memory of his recent outpouring, both emotional and liquid, engenders in him a sensation not unlike indigestion of the brain. *How can I ever face Lexie again?* he wonders while at the same time consuming several large pieces of chocolate hazelnut fudge. Yet to never again sit in the kitchen and watch Lexie julienne his favorite vegetables is certainly also a less-than-appealing alternative. *And,* he reminds himself, *I really did enjoy the oolong.*

━•••━

Lexie gazes at the empty chair so recently occupied by her employer. She stretches out her hand as if to touch in comfort the slightly damp remembered visage. She replays the conversation in her mind, still amazed at its content. How strange and wonderful that John Frederick would share with her the gift of need. Smiling, Lexie pours herself a cup of cooling oolong.

Chapter 14

What a Beautiful Morning, Oh!

John Frederick maneuvers himself into his place at the kitchen table. It has been a week since his last incursion, and after much soul searching and mouth stuffing, he has decided that the best course of action is to pretend that his and Lexie's last face-to-face communication involved nothing more than a simple exchange of cordial pleasantries.

"Good morning, my dear Lexie," he says, hoping she will be similarly inclined.

Her response seems to convey her tacit agreement. "What a beautiful day," she says, nodding at the window.

"Oh what a beautiful morning," he responds. The tune falls softly from his mouth. "Sorry," he says. "My parents went to the theater a lot and always brought back the cast recordings. Someone says something and the lyrics just pop into my head."

"No, it's wonderful," Lexie says. "My mother used to take

me to see every musical that came to town. Of course, you'd need an oxygen mask to reach our seats."

"I've got a beautiful feeling . . ." The air fills with sound of John Frederick's tenor and Lexie's clear soprano voices, somehow harmonious, and spontaneously joyful.

"The world is alive with the sound of music," John Frederick croons.

"But the rain in Spain falls mainly in the plain," Lexie adds.

"Here's one I bet you don't know," John Frederick teases, although slightly awestruck by this unaccustomed easy exchange. "Who am I? Was it all planned in advance . . . ?"

Lexie is quick to chime in: "Leonard Bernstein's *Peter Pan*. Not the one with Mary Martin."

They laugh, and then there is a moment of silence. The music still hangs in the air between them.

Chapter 15

John Frederick and *The King and I*

John Frederick wakes up smiling. Today is *The King and I* day. He is looking forward to the music, the ambience, and, of course, the food. He and Lexie have discussed the menu at length. Although Thailand is, unfortunately, one of those places he has not actually visited, he has sampled exotic Thai/Siamese delicacies at several restaurants in New York and at a small, but highly touted, four-table hideaway in a strip mall in Hollywood's famed Thai Town.

Now up and about, John Frederick hums softly as he painstakingly pulls on purple silk pants gathered at the waist and ankles. Nothing like having one of Broadway's most talented *costumiers* on retainer, he congratulates himself, reaching for the accompanying short black tone-on-tone jacket. Of course, in *The King and I*, this would have been worn bare over Yul Brynner's manly chest, but John Frederick has decided to forgo cinematic authenticity and wear a flesh-colored body shirt that will, he is sure, maintain the effect while leaving him comfortably encased. A bald cap, donned to approximate Yul Brynner's shaved head, completes the ensemble.

John Frederick turns slowly in front of the mirror. He is confident Lexie will be pleased and surprised by his efforts. Indeed, he had considered ordering a surprise costume for Lexie as well, but upon reflection had concluded that cooking a gourmet meal while wearing a corset and hoop skirt would tax even Lexie's considerable culinary talents.

John Frederick slowly descends the stairs, accompanied by the sound of rustling silk and periodic groans. Thanks to his recent bouts of exercise and hiking, he makes it to the formal dining room with only moderate huffing and puffing and a heated red flush on his face that he is confident will have abated before Lexie's arrival. John Frederick has given her strict instructions concerning the day, and has forbidden her to enter the formal dining room until the appointed time. The suspense is now palpable.

When Lexie at last enters from the kitchen, she stops cold and stares at the room around her. Her eyes widen, and for a moment there is silence. John Frederick feels as if he is standing beneath a spotlight. Then Lexie smiles, and he releases the breath he didn't even realize he was holding.

"Oh, John Frederick, this is . . . amazing. Everything is so . . . in *character*. Even your outfit!"

John Frederick happily registers that Lexie appears to be only minimally disconcerted by the sight of a colorfully garbed, large, bald man standing in front of her, and that, judging by the soft giggle that escapes from her mouth, she is at least entertained by the transformation.

"And I can't believe you brought in all these oriental rugs. And the silk draping for the ceiling. Wherever did you get it?"

"It's from my mother's antique sari collection. I must confess poor Mrs. Floyd nearly had apoplexy, but I think in the end even she admired the effect," he says, so pleased by Lexie's expression of appreciation that his face threatens to flush red again, albeit this time from delight rather than exertion.

⤙ • ⤚

John Frederick is even more pleased when Lexie continues to smile, between her own delicate sips, as he slurps his tom kha gai with gusto—such a wonderful soup, the perfect combination of coconut milk and lemongrass. The pad thai that follows is another masterpiece, the complex mixture of pan-fried rice noodles, peanuts, and tamarind providing a rainbow of taste sensations. The Thai ice tea, and Lexie's company, serve as the perfect complement.

"Lexie, Lexie, you are a marvel," he says as he pauses in between bites.

"Thank you. It is a pleasure to cook for you, especially since I've gotten a chance to know you."

Thus prompted—by chance or Lexie's intuition, he isn't sure—John Frederick begins to sing "Getting to Know You," one of his favorite selections from *The King and I*. Lexie joins in, just as she has during their morning repasts—softly at first, but then with vocal enthusiasm of a true aficionado.

John Frederick pauses as they finish the final chorus, then says, "Let's start from the beginning, shall we?" and pushes a button on the console behind him, thus liberating the music from the confines of his cleverly hidden audio system.

And so, to the strains of Rodgers and Hammerstein's beloved musical, together, they sing their way through the evening. John Frederick is pleased to learn that Lexie can even whistle.

Chapter 16

The Heart Attack

The sky is bright blue, streaked with wisps of cloud. John Frederick's senses are filled with the essence of morning as he races by on a shiny black bicycle: newly crisped bacon lying on a white paper towel, the grease sinking into the soft fold of paper; the glugging sound of maple syrup flowing from its bottle onto fluffy golden pancakes; the splash of milk as it hits the awaiting flakes.

The wind rushes past his face, the handlebars feel firm between his hands, his knees pump in a rhythm. That John Frederick has never successfully ridden a bicycle and that there is no way a bicycle saddle could accommodate his girth is of no import. This is a dream, and in dreams the laws of logic and physics are null and void.

John sees Lexie waiting for him in the distance. She is wearing a white dress that billows in the breeze, and she is holding a picnic basket. John Frederick begins to pedal faster and faster, but the distance between him and the red-haired vision does not diminish. The road, which was just a moment ago flat and inviting, now seems to tilt upward.

John Frederick catches a glimpse of something in the rear-view circular mirror attached to his right handlebar. It is large and looming and coming closer. Surely nothing that huge, that bulky, could run so fast on the small legs poking out from beneath its enormous bulbous shape . . . and yet it is gaining on him.

Suddenly the clouds darken, and raindrops hit his skin like liquid daggers. John Frederick begins to pedal even more frantically. His legs strain and his heart beats in a pounding rhythm that echoes the falling torrents of water. He clenches his jaw, and a jolt of pain runs up his arm. He is pedaling so fast that everything around him is a blur except for the monster that continues to move in on him, drawing closer and closer until he can almost feel its short, stubby fingers reaching for his neck. A shaft of lightning crashes through the sky, illuminating the surroundings with a blinding light.

John Frederick opens his eyes and blinks in the glaring sunlight streaming through the window. He feels only pain and confusion. He manages to push the button on the side of his headboard as he falls, unconscious, into encroaching darkness.

⋙•⋘

Lexie awakens to the unaccustomed sound of feet and voices, and an unanticipated sense of foreboding. As she rushes into the hallway, the voices become clearer.

"I don't know how we're going to get him down from the bedroom. There's an elevator off the bedroom, but it just isn't big enough for the Poppa Bear gurney."

"Do we know if old PB is big enough to hold him? Man, I'm glad the department pays for medical insurance, because I sure as hell am going to bust something carrying that guy down the stairs."

"Well, we better figure out something fast. We've got to get this guy to the hospital before there's permanent damage."

It takes a moment for Lexie to realize that the voices are coming from a group of uniformed men standing at the bottom of the grand stairway. They are surrounded by paraphernalia that, based on bits of memory from a television show Lexie used to watch with her mother, she identifies as emergency medical equipment. With that flash of recognition comes the realization that the men are referring to John Frederick, who at this very moment must be in some sort of physical distress. How can they stand there and make derogatory comments about his size when, as trained emergency personnel, they should be rushing to his aid?

Lexie bursts into the foyer. "Please, you've got to help him." And then, more forcefully, "Get him down those stairs immediately."

Lexie wonders who's giving the command, completely unaware that this strong, authoritative voice is hers. Mrs. Floyd, who has been talking on the phone to John Frederick's personal physician, drops the receiver in astonishment.

The emergency medical team races up the stairs, carrying the largest stretcher assembly Lexie has ever seen. She follows, but forces herself to stop at the top landing. There is just not enough room for anyone else, and now that the paramedics have finally rediscovered their routine, she does not want to in any way impede their progress.

"On my count of three, we roll him onto the sheet," one of the firemen says. "Okay now. One, two, three." Lexie hears grunting sounds and the creaking of the bed frame.

"All right. We're going to do this. There's six of us. We can handle it. One. Two. Three. Lift."

"Oh my God!" The screamed oath from one of the firemen penetrates the air, followed by the groan of straining metal.

"We did it, guys. Now all we have to do is get him down the stairs."

Six sweating, panting men emerge from the bedroom, three on each side of the gurney. John Frederick's unconscious body flows over the edge of the stretcher, pushing against the men's forearms as they maneuver their burden towards the stairs.

When the group passes her, Lexie can see the slight rise and fall of John Frederick's chest. It forms a rhythmic counterpoint to the side-to-side sway of his belly as the firemen carry their charge down the stairway. There is nothing more she can do now except follow John Frederick to the hospital and wait for the outcome.

Chapter 17

John Frederick
Is Floating

*J*ohn Frederick is floating. He is thoroughly enjoying the sensation—he feels rather like one of those giant balloons floating above the Macy's Parade. This feeling is further enforced by the long silver thread that is apparently tethering him to the ground. When he glances down, however, rather than the teeming sidewalks of Manhattan, John Frederick sees only a tiny room far below him. The space is filled with people who appear to be leaning over a large white mound in the center of the room. The green of their clothing makes splotches of contrast against the white.

For reasons that are unclear to him, John Frederick finds the scene disconcerting, and he lifts his gaze toward a shining brightness that has materialized in front of him. In the middle of this light, he sees a gauzy, white figure holding out a beckoning hand. Beside the figure is the largest confection John Frederick has ever seen. It is somewhat like a wedding cake, covered in white icing and marzipan flowers. He knows that this cake will taste of every flavor that he has ever enjoyed: chocolate, strawberry, carrot, hazelnut, mocha, dark fudge, and, more miraculously, filet mignon, sole almondine, and smoked salmon. John Frederick begins to float towards this amazing vision. He feels very, very happy.

But then he hears a faint noise coming from far away. It is the sound of someone crying. John Frederick wishes they would stop, because they are interfering with his smooth passage toward what seems to be the culmination of all his dreams. And yet there is something compelling about the sound. He hears the whisper of a name—*"Lexie, Lexie"*—and he begins to remember. He remembers her smile, her voice, and the wonderful dishes she has created just for him. Yes, Lexie. He would very much like to talk to her and tell her about how he can float and how welcoming the light is. But he knows that is impossible, and all at once, he feels very sad.

Chapter 18

The Waiting Room

*T*hey wait in a gray-green room decorated with pictures of sunflowers; Lexie, Mrs. Floyd, and even Caleb Mayfield sit motionless. Caleb's voice breaks the silence.

"I remember the first time I met John Frederick. I was around twelve, and my father was John Frederick Senior's business manager. The two of them decided that since John Frederick and I were about the same age, we might become friends. It was a disaster, of course. John Frederick looked at me with such a look of superiority and disdain, I decided I never wanted to see him again. Funny how things change."

"Please," Mrs. Floyd pleads, "no remembrances now. It feels too much like a wake. We don't know yet what's going to happen."

Silence returns. All time has stopped. There is no past, no future, only the interminable present. Lexie has stopped looking at the round white clock with the large black numbers because she knows the hands will be fixed in the same position as the last time she dared lift her head to gaze at it.

Once again she feels the tears leaking from her closed eyelids. They trail down her cheek with a slithery sensation. How can her teardrops be moving if time has stopped? She utters a prayer so soft that it becomes one with the faint whisper of the air conditioning—"Please, please, let him come back."

"I will make him the most wonderful welcome home cake," she adds. "It will be the biggest cake I have ever made, and I will decorate it with birds, roses, and musical notes." Mentally she begins to assemble all the ingredients and lines them up on the kitchen counter. She is deciding what flavorings and spices to add when the doors at the end of the waiting room swing open and Dr. Mathews emerges through them, looking grave.

No, no, I won't listen, Lexie vows. But she cannot keep the doctor's words from penetrating her consciousness.

"We've dodged a bullet. John Frederick has had a massive heart attack, but he is going to pull through. However, a lot of things have to change if we want to avoid an encore. There are some big lifestyle changes that have to be implemented, including a new exercise regimen and a complete change in his eating habits. We've got to get that weight off."

Lexie feels lightheaded with relief. A vision pops into her head of the four of them standing in front of John Frederick, each holding a shovel. They dig into his massive body, shoveling off great globs of fat and putting them into a neat pile. These will, of course, be made into little fat jackets that will be donated to all the starving children in third-world countries around the globe.

Lexie is interrupted mid-dig by the continuing discussion of John Frederick's future.

"Each one of you must be involved in John Frederick's return to health," Dr. Mathews says.

"What do I need to do in terms of Mr. Frederick's living arrangements?" Mrs. Floyd asks without pause.

Lexie duly notes the appropriateness of the adverb.

"I would suggest that in the early stages, he stay in an easily accessible area, one that doesn't involve stairs. That will make it less stressful for all of you, as well as for John Frederick."

"That won't be a problem," Mrs. Floyd responds.

Lexie can see that being given something positive to do has helped restore Mrs. Floyd's equilibrium. As the housekeeper's back straightens and the color returns to her face, Lexie can only hope that any instructions sent in her direction will have a similar restorative effect.

Dr. Mathews now turns toward Caleb, who, anticipating the doctor's concern, begins to speak.

"I don't actually live on the premises, but I can still be your liaison to Frederick House. I'll provide overall coordination and oversee finding the necessary medical equipment and temporary staff."

The doctor nods his head in acknowledgment. Lexie knows her assignment is coming next.

"And you, Ms. Haynes, are perhaps the most critical element in John Frederick's recovery," he says. "I'll be depending upon you to see that the patient's diet is properly restricted and monitored. Of course, the hospital can provide you with a list of recommended food plans, recipes, and healthy-heart cookbooks."

Contrary to Lexie's hopes, rather than feeling uplifted by the doctor's remarks, she finds herself sinking through the floor. How can she possibly satisfy John Frederick's eclectic appetite without free rein to create the most complicated and filling dishes? What can she give him to fill the void?

"Thank you," she mutters. If only she could go back to shoveling.

Chapter 19

Alien Abduction

Once again, John Frederick is floating. His thoughts trail after him in the inky darkness. *Where is my body this time? Where is my cake?* And, *Wait, didn't I just settle all this?* As he continues to float, he notices that unlike before, he is not feeling light and buoyant but rather dense and heavy, ferried through the darkness by some external craft. *Yes,* he decides, *I definitely do have a body.*

To confirm this, John Frederick tries to lift one leaden eyelid. After an eternity of effort, he feels a slight tightening of his eye muscle and his lid begins to lift.

The light is dazzling—too dazzling, the opposite of the beautiful white light he remembers. This makes him want to descend back into darkness, and so he does.

♦ • ♦

Eons later, John Frederick again opens his eyes. This time he is prepared for the light, but not for what it illuminates. Even through only partially focused eyes, he can tell he is in a dauntingly open space without the safe impermeability of walls or doors, totally exposed to anyone who might pass by. Furthermore, this area is filled with machines, screens, tubes, and pumps, accompanied by a cacophony of beeps, whirring noises, voices, and the sound of incessant footsteps.

I am either asleep and having the worst nightmare of my life, John Frederick thinks, *or I am dead and in hell.* Remembering his earlier sensation of being carried by a floating vessel, he wonders if he has indeed been ferried—across the river Styx, by Charon, to the entryway of the underworld.

There is, of course, a third alternative—that he has been kidnapped by aliens—but John Frederick dismisses this as being patently too absurd. However, as his eyes continue to focus, he discovers, to his complete horror, that his body has sprouted an array of tubes and wires that stretch from his flesh to the mechanical devices surrounding him. There are also strangely garbed individuals moving quickly in and out of the giant room and up and down the corridor. Perhaps he actually has been the object of an alien abduction.

"Help!" he shouts, but nothing emerges but a hoarse gurgle. The space in his mouth and throat that is normally open and available for producing speech is filled with a large tube, the other end of which is attached to a large machine that's moving to an up-and-down rhythm curiously like breathing.

One of the aliens trots over to his side. "I see you are awake."

"No, I'm not," John Frederick says—or at least, that is what he intends the sounds he makes to mean. To emphasize this fact, he closes his eyes.

"That's right," says the alien—who is, curiously, speaking perfect English. "You just rest now. There's no need to be frightened. You're in the hospital, in the critical care unit. You've had a serious heart attack, but you're getting the best care possible."

John Frederick can feel a tide of panic rising up his spine. Nightmares, hell, spaceships, those are things with which he can cope—but betrayal by his own physical being is beyond the pale.

"You mustn't stress yourself," the alien adds. "I'll just adjust the level of sedation."

She does something to one of the tubes, and a warm, comforting wave flows through John Frederick's body.

Clearly this has indeed been a dream; tomorrow, everything will be normal.

Chapter 20

A Night in the Garden

*L*exie is sitting propped up in her bed in her yellow room at Frederick House. The house is dark and silent except for the sounds of the old house as it settles itself, and the sniffling sound of her breath.

"Why am I still crying?" she asks the walls. "John Frederick is going to be all right. He's coming home tomorrow." The room provides no answer. "Buck up, girl," she whispers, but this exhortation banishes neither fears nor tears. Lexie knows that John Frederick is, in fact, not all right, and that although he has survived the immediate crisis, the future is as unilluminated as the shadowy walls of her room.

She remembers that day when she crept uninvited into John Frederick's room and then ran from him, screaming in fright at his looming bulk. *When did he become so dear to me?* Lexie wonders. Looking back upon her actions and reactions during his heart attack and its aftermath, she is now achingly aware that losing John Frederick has come to mean so much more to her than losing her job or even banishment from her yellow room.

Somewhere in her time at Frederick House, the massive flesh that used to seem so oppressively large has become simply the shape of John Frederick. His voice, so stern during their initial encounter, is now a source of song, laughter, praise, and appreciation. Lexie smiles at the revelation that John Frederick has given meaning to her life. Then reality returns, and John Frederick's deteriorated health wipes away any feeling of peace.

Resigned to the fact that this night will bring no restful sleep, Lexie swings her legs over the side of the bed and snuggles her feet into her worn leather slip-ons. It is too soon to begin the day's work, and in any event, she finds herself reluctant to head for the kitchen, where the ghosts of happy melodies will contrast so jarringly with the mood of the hour. Instead she crosses through the darkened house and out into the moon-streaked night. As she descends the steps to the garden, the smell of blossoms and greenery floats through the air and slides into her nostrils.

Lexie sits down on the stone edging, her knees drawn up to her chest and her hands clasped around her shins. She can almost see the thoughts circling round and round inside her head like cyclists in a velodrome. *How can I help him? I have to help him. What should I do?* But as she continues to rest her head on her knees, the garden scents begin to calm her mind and body, and her thoughts slowly ride off toward gentler destinations, both present and past.

Eight-year-old Lexie sits by the fire, a temporarily abandoned copy of Edward Eager's Half Magic *forming a miniature tent on the floor beside her. Shifting her gaze from the fire to her father, she asks, "Poppa, is fire the same as magic?"*

Lexie's father looks up from his book. "No, my question girl. There's magic in it, but it's not the fire itself. Fire is just a chemical reaction."

Lexie enters the kitchen, where her mother is mixing the dough that will soon become chocolate chip cookies laced with peanut butter. "Momma, is cooking magic?"

Her mother smiles. "Perhaps, in a way. But I think it's really more about art, experimentation, and intuition. You certainly know about intuition."

Lexie nods, proud that she understands big words like "intuition" and "chemical reaction."

A few moments later, sitting on her special stone steps at the back of the yard, Lexie directs her inquiry to the small purple flower peeping out from between the stones. "What is magic?" she asks, not really expecting an answer. Then a much more compelling thought blots out the thread of her inquiries: if she wants the cookies while they are still warm and gooey, she must immediately return to the kitchen. Scampering back to the house, she is only dimly aware of the voice of the wind calling after her, "It's you."

Back in the present, Lexie opens her eyes, unsure as to time or place, but the hard feel of stone beneath her rear end encourages her to stand, stretch, and reclaim her bearings. Her dream memories disappear with each blink of her eyelids.

"I can't believe I actually fell asleep on a rock when I couldn't get comfortable in a warm bed," she says aloud, yawning. "And that it's morning already."

Back inside, Lexie runs through her morning routine, starting with a quick wake-up shower. She pours a small dollop of soap onto the net bath sponge, then splashes on the water. She runs the sponge across her arm absentmindedly, watching as the water blooms the soap into an expanding foamy lather, and then gently washes it away.

A sudden thought pierces her brain. *This is how I've been creating meals for John Frederick. All my focus has been on expansion, the adding of flavors and scents and portions. But from now on, I will focus on subtraction, reduction. I can help John Frederick rebalance his body. I know I can. I will make him well.* Inspired, Lexie can almost feel spikes of energy radiating throughout her body.

Invigoration stays with Lexie as she completes her cleansing, drying, and dressing and heads into the kitchen. She is almost certain she can actually feel the energy coalescing into her fingertips, flowing down the spoon, and swirling into the simmering pot that holds the ingredients of John Frederick's homecoming meal.

Chapter 21

The Magic Room— Home at Last

*J*ohn Frederick drifts slowly back into consciousness. The room feels strange. He knows he is no longer in the hospital. It is too quiet and the smells are wrong. In fact, the smells are vaguely familiar. They remind him of his childhood. But this is not his room. He can tell by the way the air curves around the space. It is too small for his room.

He opens his eyes and memory comes flooding back. He is indeed back at Frederick House, having been liberated from the hospital yesterday afternoon. He realizes that he is in the first-floor guest room in the east wing of the house, and furthermore he is dressed in his bright-orange pajamas, having read some-where that orange is the color of healing, not to mention the shade of his favorite sweet potato soufflé.

"I'm afraid you won't be able to be in your own room right now," he remembers Mrs. Floyd explaining. "The guest room is so much more convenient. There are no stairs, and access is so much simpler."

The guest room. As a boy, the guest room was a room of mystery, forbidden yet alluring. It was a magical room, empty until it conjured up someone not part of the usual household coterie. John Frederick would sneak into the hallway and crouch beside the marble table with the huge vase that was part of the magic ritual. If the vase was empty, the room would remain empty and locked. If the vase was filled with colorful blooms and greenery, the door would open and some stranger would emerge from the room, fully formed and dressed for the day.

In those long-gone childhood days, John Frederick would wonder what the strangers did when they were not being man-ifested by the magic room. Perhaps they lived in a magic world full of genies and giants; they might even *be* genies or giants.

And now the adult John Frederick is himself sleeping in the magic room. John Frederick still thinks of the guest room in this manner, even though he long ago realized that this is a very ordinary room and that the visitors came from the outside into the room and not the other way around.

As John Frederick lies in his bed, he wishes that the room actually was full of magic. Then he could simply lie there and wait for the miraculous spell that would restore his health and eliminate any danger of future heart problems. If the room were truly magic he could continue to live his life fully, in the gastro-nomic as well as every other sense of the word, and the size of his body and his life would have no detrimental impact on his health. But even in his fantasies John Frederick knows this is too much to wish for.

Chapter 22

Chocolate Soup

*L*exie walks slowly across the floor, carrying her tray like an acolyte approaching the holy sanctum. As she walks, she can hear the sound of liquid sloshing against the sides of the soup tureen, and the slightest hint of vegetables and warm broth floats towards her nostrils.

Reaching her destination at last, Lexie balances the tray against the edge of the small table next to the door. A large urn of flowers has already laid claim to most of the space, but there is just enough room so that she can secure the tray's position by bracing it with her hip.

As Lexie looks up at the door, she notices her hand is trembling, moved by a combination of excitement, anxiety, and suppressed joy. She curls her hand into a fist and raps on the door.

"John Frederick, it's Lexie. Can I come in?"

Hearing a muffled noise from the interior, Lexie turns the handle, pushes the door inward, and maneuvers her body and the tray into the room.

John Frederick is sitting partially upright in the bed, his

back against a mound of pillows. He is wearing bright-orange pajamas and looks rather like a large pumpkin. Lexie swallows the beginnings of a nervous laugh and moves towards the bed.

"Oh, John Frederick, it is so good to see you again. They wouldn't let me visit you in the hospital, but I waited outside the day they brought you in until I was sure you were okay."

"It's all right. I knew you were there."

"You did?"

"I could hear you crying."

"But John Frederick, I was in the waiting room the whole time. I never got any closer to you than that."

"Well, I wasn't exactly stationary."

Lexie is beginning to feel a bit confused. "You mean they moved you to another bed?"

"No, it was something else. Maybe I shouldn't tell you any more. You'll think I'm crazy."

Now Lexie is both confused and concerned. If John Frederick, her beloved but quintessential eccentric, thinks something is crazy, it must be off the charts.

"Please, John Frederick, don't stop."

"Well, for part of the time I was floating—not from anesthesia, but really floating. I could see and hear everything around me and for a considerable distance beyond that. It was quite wonderful. In front of me was this beautiful white light, and beside it the most glorious, ornate cake that I knew would taste of chocolate and every flavor I have ever loved. I thought about moving towards the light and the cake, but then something pulled me back. It was the sound of your tears."

Lexie's eyes widen. "But John Frederick, that's incredible. While I was in the waiting room I thought about making you a huge, amazing cake. All I wanted was for you to come home safely."

"And here I am, so I guess you know what I chose in the end," John Frederick says softly. And then, pointing at the tray, "But that doesn't look like a cake plate."

Lexie lifts off the lid of the tureen. "I've made you a special soup."

"Is it chocolate?"

"I don't think there is such a thing as chocolate soup."

"Well, there should be," John Frederick declares as he lifts a spoonful of the warm broth towards his mouth.

Lexie watches anxiously as John Frederick swallows the broth, licks his lips, and then smiles.

"Well, my dear Lexie. If I can't have cake or chocolate soup, this will do nicely."

Chapter 23

Brunhilde

*J*ohn Frederick is sitting on the edge of his bed in the Magic Room, wishing, among other things, that he were back in his own room and living his own life.

I know I'm supposed to feel grateful; I've been given a second chance and have returned to life, he philosophizes to himself. *But it's not my life, it's someone else's, a life constrained by limits. There is a whole team of "theys" who are beginning to dictate the parameters of my life: how I must act, what I must do, and worst of all, what I must eat. How I wish I could go back to that wonderful light and that enticing cake. It isn't fair. What have I done to deserve this? I am a kind man, a man who loves music and books. Why am I being punished this way?*

There is a knock on the door and John Frederick knows that it is one of the "theys" coming to impose some cleverly designed restriction or unpleasant task. He mutters, "Come in," aware that the person outside the door, whoever they might be, will come in anyway, and at least this way he can pretend to be the instigator of the contact.

The door opens and in strides the worst of the "theys," Brunhilde the Valkyrie. John Frederick knows, of course, that her name isn't actually Brunhilde, and that she isn't a Valkyrie but a physical therapist/trainer. However, she is tall, blond, and large, her body wrapped in muscle and sinew. The fact that her name is Julia Petit is totally inappropriate. There is nothing "petit" about Julia. John Frederick can almost see the Viking helmet and horns, her flaxen hair growing from a smooth straight bob into long blond braids.

"Time to get up and move," says Brunhilde, smiling.

John Frederick knows that she is smiling because she soon will be pulling and stretching and pushing on his body as if he were a prisoner being questioned on the rack. At least she doesn't use the plural "we" when addressing him.

Chapter 24

The Reverse Elf

An hour later John Frederick is back in the Magic Room, Brunhilde having departed for Valhalla, or at least some other foreign land beyond the borders of Frederick House. Left once again in cherished solitude, he sits on the edge of the bed, staring at the far wall of his temporary abode. His sulky mood is tempered slightly by the welcome news—communicated by Mrs. Floyd precisely at the moment that Brunhilde started to bend his leg at an impossible angle—that he will soon be able to go back to his own room. According to Mrs. Floyd, the doctor has given the move his blessing, declaring that the danger of an imminent relapse has passed and a return to more amiable surroundings might ease the stress of his recovery.

John Frederick knows that even in his own room some things will be changed. He is aware that Mrs. Floyd is already fixing things up even as he lies here recovering from his session with the Valkyrie. He fancies he can hear the patter of foreign feet moving about his real room on the floor above.

Upstairs, Mrs. Floyd and Lexie are walking across the green patterned carpet leading to John Frederick's inner sanctum. Lexie carries a large canvas drawstring bag while Mrs. Floyd is pushing an empty serving cart. Lexie watches Mrs. Floyd as the older woman raises her hand as if to knock and then, shaking her head, quickly moves her hand to the doorknob.

"Force of habit," Mrs. Floyd says, pushing open the door. "Time to begin the sanitizing process."

Lexie nods, looking about the room. She still feels a bit like a trespasser even though she is here at Mrs. Floyd's insistence. "The fact that he trusts you might make this a bit easier on him," Mrs. Floyd explained with uncharacteristic openness. Lexie recognizes this as a sign that Mrs. Floyd has not yet quite recovered from the alarming events of the recent past.

Of course, the sanitizing mission upon which they are embarking does not involve banishing germs but the much more deadly danger of caloric temptations. Lexie isn't sure that John Frederick would want anyone, even her, to make such changes, but is somewhat comforted by the fact her actions will at least be consistent with her newly embraced philosophy of culinary subtraction.

Mrs. Floyd moves toward the dressing area and closet, while Lexie turns to tackle the shelves. These are overflowing with books and other treasures, a testimony to John Frederick's eclectic mind. The largest section is, not unexpectedly, devoted to all aspects of gastronomy, including volumes on the history of agriculture and food cultivation, numerous Michelin guides, and one whole shelf weighted down with bound volumes of *Bon Appétit* dating back to its inaugural edition in 1955. Lexie can't help but smile as she picks up one of the well-thumbed Michelin guides, its margins filled with John Frederick's handwritten commentary. His notes are heavily supplemented with underlining and exclamation points.

"I wish it was only his curiosity that was so voracious," Lexie thinks, reaching for the boxes of imported pretzels stacked neatly against the *Encyclopedia of Bavarian Specialties*. She takes the boxes and places them inside her canvas sack. A moment later, the pretzels are joined by tins of chocolate, displaced from their customary resting place next to the *History of Chocolatiering in Belgium and the Netherlands*. The chocolates make a crunching sound as they land on the layer of pretzels at the bottom of the bag.

"I feel like a Christmas elf in reverse," Lexie murmurs as she continues to remove goodies and put them in her sack for later disposal.

"What did you say?" inquires Mrs. Floyd from inside the closet.

"Sorry, I didn't know I'd spoken out loud."

Having pondered the existence of reverse elves, Lexie expands her musings to wonder what a reverse Santa Claus would look like. Perhaps he would wear a white suit with red trim and be very thin. Although, on second thought, white would not be a very practical color for scuttling down chimneys to remove presents from under the tree. But then, the red velvet and large girth of the original Santa Claus aren't exactly suited to chimney travel either.

As Lexie continues to move around the room, she notices that John Frederick's filing system seems to have gone astray. The stack of pink pastry boxes seems to have no relation to *Famous Athlete Gourmets and Chefs*, unless John Frederick has conflated boxes with boxing. But filed properly or not, these as well as dozens of other delicacies are destined for removal, and before long, Lexie's sack is full. Although the room is still filled with books and small *objets d'art*, and even several *Star Trek* figures, the room seems denuded. Lexie knows that John Frederick will notice every empty space, every missing bag and box, and this makes her sad.

"It isn't fair," she tells the Mr. Spock replica. "I feel guilty for contributing to John Frederick's enlargement, and now I feel guilty for removing all these sources of pleasure."

In her mind, Lexie can almost hear the Vulcan's response: *"Do not waste your energy on guilt. Guilt is a useless human emotion."*

"Yes," she says. "But we are not on Vulcan."

Chapter 25

An Adventure

"Outdoors," John Frederick exclaims, regarding Brunhilde with horror. "Why do we have to go outdoors? There are perfectly good hiking trails inside." He has in fact dressed himself in his favorite red jogging outfit in anticipation of another indoor stroll.

"The fresh air will be good for you."

John Frederick continues to stare at Brunhilde with disbelief. Doesn't she understand that outside is something one views through glass, or at most passes through quickly while moving between one enclosed space to another?

"You must have spent time outside when you were little . . . er, *younger*," Brunhilde says.

John Frederick does recall some moments from his early childhood when he would go outside to the garden to play. He would conjure up monsters and pirates while Nanny Brown sat on the stone bench reading her book. But when he learned to read—which he did at a very early age—he quickly found that the adventures suggested by those printed lines were infinitely more rewarding than those that could be found in the garden. That must be why Nanny Brown never went outside without a book.

Certainly, John Frederick would never acknowledge his primal fear that the outside is where people go to disappear. He knows that this is not literally true, of course, just as he knows that the Magic Room is not where people are conjured into being. Nonetheless, his distaste for the outdoors is profound.

It is thus with great apprehension that John Frederick finds himself walking down the stone steps at the rear of the house, his body supported by Brunhilde on one side and the stone wall on the other. He tries to distract himself by pondering how Brunhilde became such a complete "they."

"Look how far you've come," Brunhilde says.

Indeed, while his mind has been occupied making excursions into Brunhilde's mythical history, John Frederick has mysteriously moved across the surrounding walkway and into the garden. Like his favorite cartoon character who, suddenly finding himself halfway across an abyss, plummets to the ground, John Frederick begins to slip down toward the grass.

"Oh no," he cries, imagining himself slipping farther and farther until he is embedded in the grass. Future generations will come and perch on his semiburied head and tell each other, "This used to be John Frederick before the cruel Brunhilde forced him to walk outside."

The same Brunhilde, however, saves John Frederick from his future existence as a picnic table by forcibly pushing him onto the very stone bench that once provided support for Nanny Brown's posterior.

"Thank you," he says, both to Brunhilde and the ghost of Nanny Brown.

As he sinks gratefully onto the bench, John Frederick inhales the multitextured scents of the garden, along with a whiff of newly mowed grass. This moment of outdoor tolerance is immediately swept away by the realization that the only way to return to his indoor sanctuary is to continue walking.

"Can't we get the electric cart?" he asks. "I think I feel faint."

"It's not that far back to the house," Brunhilde says. "I suspect that you walk farther than this when you go from your room to the kitchen."

"Yes, but that is not outside, and there is usually food involved."

Chapter 26

"'Ome"

"Well, at least now I have something to show for all that torture," John Frederick mutters as he begins his climb up the stairs leading to his bedroom. At last the "theys," the terrible "theys," are letting him back into his old room. To be home again after all his travails and travels, his treks through the halls and corridors of Frederick House, and then, yesterday, the wilderness of the great outdoors.

John Frederick pauses at the landing halfway up the stairs. What an achievement; he has made it all the way up without a stop. He is practically flying. He rests his hand momentarily on the banister, the polished walnut smooth and warm against his palm. He tightens his grip and propels himself up to the next step.

At last John Frederick reaches the door to his room. His breathing is somewhat ragged from the exertion—and, perhaps, anticipation. As his respiration slows he begins to softly sing the lyrics from *My Fair Lady* about how loverly it would be to have a home somewhere. In deference to Eliza Doolittle's cockney accent he drops the "h," reducing the word to "'ome." "Some people chant "ohm" to relax, he muses, but this is probably just a coincidence.

He turns the handle and pushes against the door. Something is wrong. The room smells odd, no faint aroma of snacks or pastries. His view expands with the opening door. His voice stops midlyric. The room has been more than changed, it has been burglarized, desecrated. There are empty spaces, empty shelves, missing colors.

John Frederick collapses onto his bed, overcome with shock and loss. He buries his face in the covers. For the second time in his memory the tears begin to flow.

Chapter 27

Rags

*J*ohn Frederick sits down at the kitchen table. Lexie greets him with a smile as she lowers the blades of an old-fashioned eggbeater into a large blue bowl. From his seated position, John Frederick cannot see the actual contents of the bowl.

"What are you cooking today, my dear?" he asks.

"My special lemon meringues."

"And where is the pie part?" John Frederick can't help but ask this even though he knows that gooey deserts are no longer a part of his daily menu.

"It's just the meringues, but you'll like them," Lexie says. "Wait and see."

John Fredericks lapses into silence, mesmerized by the whirring rotation of the eggbeater. After a moment, something frothy becomes visible over the edge of the bowl. Against the shiny blue ceramic, the white froth looks like clouds against a winter sky, or perhaps even snow.

"Snow," John Frederick says out loud.

"What?"

"It looks like snow." *And that is what I feel like*, he thinks. The pounds are dropping off him like snow dripping from the trees after winter thaw. But whereas trees form a solid foundation upon which the snow can accumulate, John Frederick can sense nothing inside him except hollowness. He wonders where his tree is. He looks up at Lexie. "I am truly out of sorts today. I feel so out of sync."

"Perhaps some music will help."

"Yes, a nice musical comedy is just the thing. I will go up and find the perfect musical to lift my spirits."

Back up in his room, John Frederick opens a wooden file drawer and gazes at the contents. Inside, carefully sorted, are all the theater programs his parents had brought back for him when he was a boy. John Frederick moves his fingers across the stiff cardboard edge of the file dividers, each crowned with the appropriate letter of the alphabet.

"*Annie,*" he mutters. "Heavens no. *Camelot.* Perhaps. *Funny Girl.* No, the best part is the female lead, and dressing in drag is simply too undignified. *Hello, Dolly.* Same problem."

He continues shuffling through the collection. "*The Sound of Music.* That won't work without a horde of children."

John Frederick's fingers stop and begin moving back up to the front of the alphabet. "*Oliver! Oklahoma.* No, wait. *Oliver!*, that's the ticket. And I shall be Oliver." It does not occur to him to take on the role of Fagin even though he is an adult and Oliver a child. Fagin is a thief and a con man, and John Frederick wishes to be morally and spiritually uplifted. Besides is he not too an orphan?

Having made the difficult choice of theatrical production and role, John Frederick moves over to his dressing room. There is nothing in the costume rack that seems appropriate, but since he now has an ample selection of oversized clothes that no longer fit, he turns instead to that section of the closet. Some of these garments will, of course, be altered, but the vast majority will be donated to some worthy charity. John Frederick imagines legions of girthful men dressed as John Frederick look-alikes. It is a disconcerting vision.

Focused once again on the task at hand, John Frederick reaches in and grabs a handful of white linen. This is one of his former leisure outfits—a loose top and drawstring pants, which he had thought would be perfect for strolling down a tropical beach, piña colada in hand. That he has yet to stroll down any beach, tropical or otherwise, is immaterial. It is important to be prepared.

Taking a pair of scissors from his desk drawer, John Frederick begins cutting random holes and slashes in the top and pants, stopping only to ponder the fact that both scissors and pants are both plurals, although each noun refers to a single entity.

Now for the dirt. This is provided by a small potted plant seated on the window ledge. This is John Frederick's one concession to Mother Nature, and to the supposed beneficial effect of greenery on the oxygen content of a room. He reaches into the pot, retrieves a handful of slightly damp soil, and randomly sprinkles it over the now-shredded linen. Finally, in search of verisimilitude, John Frederick smears several brown streaks across his face. This whole process is contrary to his usual preference for the pristine, but he knows one must make sacrifices for one's art.

◆●◆

"My goodness," Lexie exclaims when John Frederick enters the kitchen.

"Oliver Twist from *Oliver!*," he says by way of explanation.

In response, Lexie begins singing "As Long as He Needs

Me," which John Frederick finds rather touching, although he generally judges the heroine as a bit too subservient.

"Lovely," he says as Lexie finishes the final verse, "but a bit sad. Perhaps we should contrast it with something more upbeat. 'Consider Yourself at Home' comes to mind."

"Oh, and then there's . . ." Lexie stops.

"'Food, Glorious Food,'" John Frederick says, filling in the gap. How could he have chosen a musical that includes a paean to endless amounts of wonderful food? He feels his good mood begin to evaporate, replaced by a return of the morning's wretched hollowness. "'Food, Glorious Food,'" he repeats, his voice filled with longing. "'Food, Glorious Food.'" This time his voice cracks with immense sadness.

And then, from the very bottom of his soul, from the depths of his being, he utters the play's immortal words: "Please, sir, can I have some more?"

Chapter 28

Invasion of the Pod People

$\mathcal{J}$ohn Frederick walks around the perimeter of his room. It is his room, filled with his books and his paintings. The sensuous coverings on the bed and chair are the same. But the shelves are no longer stacked with yellow plastic bags of cookies or pink bakery boxes, and the refrigerator is now filled with apples and carrots and chilled imported mineral waters. The dimensions seem so wrong, the spaces so out of balance.

"I love this room," John Frederick says out loud, but the words ring false. He turns toward the ornate mirror in the corner, where he can see his own image staring balefully back at him. He moves closer, but still his image seems to take up less and less space.

"I do not recognize you," he says to his reflection. "You are a pod person. Someone came over in the middle of the night and switched out my body." He realizes that this is not quite the plot of *Invasion of the Body Snatchers*, but it doesn't matter.

He remembers the words of his doctor: *"You are doing so well that we may not even need the surgery. It's quite miraculous."*

The doctor smiled proudly after saying that, but John Frederick felt like throwing up. He restrained himself only because he did not want the physician to think he was bulimic. John Frederick has no need of such stratagems. His body is simply diminishing, as if in response to some divine wish. Or perhaps Lexie's wish.

John Frederick once again looks at the pod person, this image that can't be the real John Frederick, the one he has known for much of his life. The outline of his body begins to blur, as if there is no demarcation between his own physical presence and the surrounding environment.

·•·

Lexie opens the *Heart Healthy Cookbook* and begins thumbing through the recipes, hoping for further inspiration. She has been tweaking ingredients, adding spices, and subtly altering flavors in the hopes of creating dishes that are more streamlined versions of her prior offerings. Into each creation she breathes love and caring, with a hint of reduction and health. But despite her best efforts, John Frederick has been decidedly unenthusiastic about the deletion of his favorite sauces and fats. In fact, he seems to be becoming grumpier and more dissatisfied with each passing day. She hopes today will be different.

An hour later, Lexie moves through the kitchen with her usual deftness, humming softly as she puts the finishing touches on John Frederick's breakfast. Although his footsteps now echo less loudly, Lexie can hear John Frederick as he moves toward the kitchen. The kitchen chair creaks slightly but no longer screams in panic as he lowers himself down into it.

John Frederick sits at the table, his eyes apparently fixed on the wooden surface; he does not turn his head or smile as Lexie places the tray before him. Steam still rises from the bowl of oatmeal, and the small plate of fresh fruit forms a mosaic of shapes and colors.

"It's old-fashioned oatmeal," Lexie says. "Traditional Irish oats, not instant. You can tell from the texture."

John Frederick shoves his spoon into the bowl and pushes it into his mouth. He purses his lips in distaste. "It still tastes like library paste. Who ever heard of eating oatmeal without brown sugar, raisins, and cream?"

"I'm sorry, John Frederick, but the doctor says—"

"He doesn't have to eat this glop."

All Lexie can do is nod her head in sympathy. *If only I could make everything better with a wave of some mystical spoon*, she wishes silently—but there is nothing she can do. She can fill the bowl with healing and love, but there is no way she can make oatmeal taste like cherry-chocolate cheesecake, or turn cherry-chocolate cheesecake into diet food.

"Dear John Frederick," she says out loud, "I know how difficult this is for you."

"Do you, do you really? How can you possibly know what it feels like to starve yourself, to deny yourself one of life's greatest pleasures?" He glares at Lexie. "You're probably one of those people who have never had to watch their weight in all their life. In fact, I bet you're one of those people who can eat whatever they want and never gain a pound." The accusations drip off his tongue like vinegar.

Pummeled by John Frederick's words, Lexie conjures up an image of a stick figure with orange hair balancing a plate of fettuccine Alfredo in one hand and a seven-layer fudge cake in the other. The stick figure begins to spin around so quickly that its body disappears and all that can be seen are blotches of orange, white, and dark brown.

Lexie shakes her head, her own irritation beginning to rise. "Don't you realize that small people can be uncomfortable with their bodies too? People walk by me as if I wasn't there, or pat me on the head and treat me like a child. Everything I want is out of reach. I can't tell you how often I've wanted to be taller— just a few inches, that's all."

"And that's the difference! " John Frederick shouts. "You'd welcome a change in your dimensions, while I'm being forced to change mine against my will. I hate this. Why are they making me do this? Why are *you* making me do this?" The sound of his fork slamming against his plate resounds through the kitchen like a gun salute at a funeral.

"Perhaps some tea will help calm things down," Lexie says, talking to herself as much as to John Frederick. She moves over to the tea cabinet and peers at the shelves lined with tins of fresh tea, organized by type and flavor, trying to find the perfect blend to restore harmony. She finally settles on a delicate white tea infused with orange blossoms, and waits for the water to heat.

All the while John Frederick remains silent, but the continued creaking of his chair as he shifts his position back and forth attests to his agitation.

The teakettle whispers, "I'm ready, I'm ready," and Lexie begins pouring the water over the tea leaves nestled in the strainer basket of the tea pot.

"This should do the trick," she says softly as she takes the teapot and two china cups and saucers over to the table. Then, more loudly as she sets down the tray, "Here you are: 'Tea for Two.'"

Her verbal cue brings no response from John Frederick, no answering melody. The only thing Lexie hears is the slurpy sound of swallowed tea. She tries very hard not to cry.

Time Passes— Notes Part II

FROM THE DESK OF JOHN FREDERICK

Lexie,

Thank you for all your support during these difficult times. Sometimes I forget to tell you.

John Frederick

FROM THE DESK OF JOHN FREDERICK

Lexie,

The food is not as satisfying as it used to be, but I understand that you are now working under constraints. Keep on trying.

Thank you,

John Frederick

FROM THE DESK OF JOHN FREDERICK

Lexie,

You seem to be slacking in your efforts. Please understand that I need all the help I can get.

John Frederick

FROM THE DESK OF JOHN FREDERICK

Lexie,

What happened to all your support? I don't need one more person telling me what I can and can't do.

John Frederick

Chapter 30

A Call for Help

*L*exie sits in her yellow room. The deepening twilight turns the walls a dark, rancid hue reminiscent of mustard crusted on a dirty plate. She wonders why she has not noticed this phenomenon before. Even here, in this once special room, all sense of comfort has fled.

How can it all have gone so wrong? Her communication with John Frederick has grown so sparse that it is now compressed into intermittent notes containing only words of anger or criticism. On those rare occasions when she catches a glimpse of him, her approach seems to freeze his facial muscles into an angry, distant scowl.

Perhaps Mrs. Floyd might know what has happened, but their relationship has never been one of shared confidence. Lexie's thoughts drift back toward Caleb Mayfield. Despite their infrequent contact, he has always given her the feeling that he is someone she could turn to in a time of need. After all, wasn't he the first person at Frederick House to offer her friendship, and didn't his steadfast presence in the hospital waiting room help carry her through that awful night when John Frederick collapsed?

Lexie picks up the phone sitting next to her on the nightstand. She has thought about getting a cell phone periodically, but the idea of being that accessible, that connected to outside distractions, has always outweighed the potential lure of such pocket-sized convenience. Besides, the heavy weight of the phone lends solidarity to her purpose.

She finds Caleb's number on the list of emergency numbers taped to the wall and dials it, then holds the phone next to her ear, listening to the rings and willing herself not to break the connection.

"Caleb Mayfield here."

"It's Lexie," she says with a catch in her throat. "I hope you don't mind me calling."

"Not at all. It's been too long."

"Caleb, something's wrong with John Frederick."

"Not another heart episode?" he asks anxiously.

"No, nothing like that. It's just that he's so different, so . . . not John Frederick." She pauses. "Maybe I'm just imagining things." She can't tell Caleb how John Frederick no longer radiates warmth as if from some inner glow, or how his entry into a room is no longer preceded by the scent of fresh-baked scones cooling on an iron baker's rack.

"Well, he certainly looks different. You really got him on an effective health regimen."

"It's not that," she says, her rising inflection nearly masking the faint clicking sound in the background. "It's so much more. And you're really the only one I can talk to."

"It's all right, Lexie. We can get together and talk this out. I've always told you you could come to me for advice. I'm here if you need me."

"Thank you, thank you, Caleb. Just hearing that makes me feel better."

"Shall we say next week? I can clear my schedule by then."

"I'm sure everything will be okay now," Lexie says with a hint of returning optimism. "Till next week."

Chapter 31

The Grandfather Tree

*L*exie sits on the stone bench beneath the Chinese elm tree, far from the formal garden. She leans her head against the multihued, multitextured trunk. The clean spaces where the bark has peeled away almost exactly match the color of her hair.

"Hello grandfather tree," she says. Like the stone steps of her childhood, this has become her own private place. She knows, of course, that a gardener or maintenance crew must come here sometimes, or else the arched branches of the tree would sweep the ground, and leafy fingers of green would fill the inside spaces instead of forming the gentle, light-pierced bowl that surrounds but does not engulf her.

Once she came here very early in the morning and listened to the birds as they swooped in to perch on the tree's welcoming arms. It seemed as though each bird brought a distinctive note of pure melody and laid tone upon tone until the sound was so full it almost burst her heart. That day, unscheduled because of another of John Frederick's forays, she sat there for hours while the birds and the tree enveloped her in wonder.

Today, however, is not such a day. It is Lexie's afternoon break, and the birds are silent. The intermittent breeze lifts the hair on her arms—or perhaps it is the trickle of disquiet running beneath her skin that's doing so.

"I don't think I can stand much more of this," she says to the tree—who, as always, listens patiently, ready to absorb either her pain or her joy.

The ground is soft with fallen leaves. Lexie scrapes them into a pyramid with the edge of her boot, then slips from the bench and kneels down, letting a handful of twigs and leaf edges slip between her fingers. The texture is slightly crinkly but not unpleasant. In response to some unspoken invitation, Lexie moves into a supine position, feeling the gentle support and strength of the ground beneath her, and makes leaf angels, her arms and legs moving slowly in and out. The smell of moist earth, leaves, and possibility caresses her senses. She feels as if the earth is taking her restless energy and transforming it into strength.

"Thank you," she whispers. She can feel herself getting bigger and bigger, like Alice in Wonderland after the "eat me" cake. Lexie knows that if she were to stand up she would touch the top of the tree. It is, therefore, somewhat disconcerting when she finally does lever herself upright and finds that she is still her usual four foot eleven and a half inches.

Sighing, she brushes the leaves from her body, morphing from tree person into human. "Good-bye, tree," she says, and she pats the trunk and turns back toward the house.

"Abandoning your duties again," a gruff voice interjects.

John Frederick, who has unexpectedly chosen this exact moment to appear on this exact path, angrily plucks a leaf from her hair. "Perhaps you were having a roll in the hay with Caleb."

Lexie suppresses her desire to say, *"Leaves, not hay."* She is astounded at this reincarnation of John Frederick's earlier accusation, one that she had thought was dead and buried. Why, she hadn't even seen Caleb in months. Suddenly, she remembers the strange clicks from last night's telephone conversation.

Tall tree Lexie emerges. "It's none of your damn business," she says firmly. This time there will be no plea for understanding. "I will not be treated this way any longer. I'll miss this place, I'll miss cooking and creating for you, and I'll even miss you. Or at least the old you. But no more of this. I quit."

John Frederick sputters for a moment, his face engorged with rage. "Good riddance," he shouts to her retreating back.

— • —

The house is quiet as Lexie walks down the corridor towards Mrs. Floyd's office. Lexie has put the last half hour to good use. The older woman looks up as Lexie places a neatly folded piece of white paper on the desk.

"I'm giving notice."

Mrs. Floyd looks sad but not at all startled. "I'm so sorry," she says. "If you need a reference, feel free to list me rather than John Frederick."

And then, for the first time in all the months of their acquaintance, Mrs. Floyd rises up from behind her desk and kisses Lexie softly on the cheek.

Chapter 32

Lexie at the Counter

*L*exie wipes down the luncheon counter at Annie's Healthy Living Emporium, using the organic spray from the cleaning aisle. A hint of orange oil mingles with the smell of simmering vegetable soup and lemon spice marinade.

"Hi, Norm," she says to the young man seated at the stool in front of her. "The usual?"

"Thanks, Lexie."

Lexie pivots to her left, takes a Lexie's Special Veggie Burger out of the fridge, and slides it onto the waiting grill. She spoons out a cup of soup and places it before a smiling Norm.

"Enjoy your soup," she says, returning his grin. "You're looking great."

"It's all thanks to you. Since I started eating here I've lost twenty pounds. You're amazing."

Lexie takes a moment to soak in the compliment and survey her tiny domain. She looks over at the line of people waiting to be seated. Although filled with hungry customers, no one is pushing or shoving; there are no shouts of "Get a move on, lady!" or "I was here first!" Instead, people are waiting in gentle silence or chatting amiably. Lexie catches a few snippets of conversation. "I love coming here, don't you?" "I just saw my doctor and he can't believe how many pounds I've dropped. In fact, he asked me what my secret is. I think he suspects I'm sneaking diet pills or something." "I've never been in here before, but the smell of cinnamon was so inviting I had to come in." "Cinnamon? I only smelled popcorn and cotton candy." "Chocolate," says someone else.

Lexie has gotten used to these differing olfactory perceptions. People seem to smell whatever aroma their fondest memories bring forward when they walk past her front entrance. It makes sense to her. After all, she reasons, if strong smells can evoke memories, why shouldn't the opposite be true? That this is a selective phenomenon, leaving some passersby to scurry past unaffected, is an enigma that Lexie feels no need to pursue.

Lexie hears the veggie burger's soft sizzle telling her that it is ready. She spatulas it onto the plate and places it in front of her smiling customer.

⤙•⤚

The luncheon rush now past, Lexie takes a moment to savor the quiet and sip a cup of chamomile tea. She looks over at Annie, the proprietor of Annie's Health Emporium.

"Come join me in a cup of tea." Lexie says, immediately conjuring up an image of the two of them backstroking their way across a gigantic mug of warm amber liquid.

"How goes it?" Annie asks. "You sure brought 'em in today. I wonder if we should think about doing an afternoon tea?"

Lexie, whose body has been soothed and imagination

stimulated by the tea, sees the room now filled with white table-cloth–covered tables accompanied by straight-backed chairs.

As if echoing her thoughts, Annie adds, "It would mean expanding,"

"But not too big," Lexie says. "I still have to be able to touch everything. If it's not hands-on, I don't think it will work."

The tea room begins to bulge outward, the walls pushing back to make room for huge double-deck ovens and vast caul-drons of tea being tended by small, frantically scurrying robots with gray metal eyes and red painted hair.

"Never," Lexie says as the room shrinks back to its usual shape and size.

"Sorry, I couldn't hear you," Annie says.

"Just thinking out loud."

"It's hard to believe you've been here nearly a year. With your talent, I didn't think you'd stay this long."

A year? It can't be. And yet she scarcely dreams of John Frederick and Frederick House anymore, although sometimes she sees him moving through the corridors of her somnolent imagination, usually in his old corpulent form—large, loom-ing, and yet strangely comforting, like a soft, luxurious down duvet. And once, just once, John Frederick began shrinking as she watched, shriveling into a black, scrabbling skeleton with tentacled fingers and a gaping red mouth.

Lexie shudders in remembrance and looks fondly across at Annie and the immaculate lunch counter.

"No, this is where I belong," she says, her eyes glowing with joy. "It's absolutely perfect."

Chapter 33

B. B. Bevins Comes to Call

*J*ohn Frederick paces back and forth in the foyer of Frederick house, his feet making a rhythmic tap followed by a sharp echo, with each step. He is waiting for an important visitor. Normally, John Frederick would never answer a knock on the door or respond to the intercom's buzz, but today he does not want to delay the encounter by even those few minutes it would take Mrs. Floyd to react and direct the visitor to the meeting place.

At long last the buzzer sounds. John Frederick stops mid-pace and strides toward the door. He pushes the button next to the intercom and addresses the person at the other end.

"Hello?"

"This is B. B. Bevins and I have an appointment with Mr. Frederick."

"Of course. I'll buzz you right in."

With that, B. B. Bevins strides through the door. He is a

short, round man who has brought with him a taller, thinner individual, who is carrying a very large garment bag draped across his extended arms.

BB gestures toward his companion. "Allow me to introduce my assistant, Orlando Steinberg."

John Frederick nods and begins to herd the two visitors across the foyer.

"I've set up a dressing area and a try-on space in the guest room. Follow me."

As they move down the corridor, John Frederick notices that the vase by the table is filled with flowers. The Magic Room awaits its visitors.

Inside the room is a trifold screen covered in blue toile, and a large garment rack hung with several pieces from John Frederick's "man of substance" period. John Frederick watches with eager anticipation as Orlando carefully hangs the garment bag on the rack.

"Mr. Frederick, I hope I may congratulate you on your impressive weight loss," BB says. "I could hardly believe it when I got your latest measurements."

John Frederick does not reply.

BB turns toward the garment rack and continues, "I must say, Mr. Frederick, that this was one of the most challenging projects in my career. Light, breathable, easy to put on and take off, and something that looks completely natural. I must say it's much easier to design something like this for the stage. Thank heavens for modern technology. Now why don't you go behind the screen and take off your clothes so we can give it a test drive."

John Frederick heads behind the screen and begins removing his shirt. In his haste, his fingers fumble with his buttons. The sound of a zipper being undone indicates the garment bag has been opened, and a moment later a hand reaches around the side of the screen. It is holding what looks like a massive and very puffy flesh-colored jacket.

"I've made this in two pieces, a top and bottom, since you won't be using a dresser. They attach to each other with Velcro."

John Frederick takes the proffered jacket. It is, indeed, lightweight, with a soft, yielding texture. He pushes his finger against the fabric, and it promptly envelops the extended digit. Encouraged, John Frederick slips one arm and then another into the garment, then closes the front opening by pressing on the Velcro tabs. He is delighted by the fact that his arms no longer hang straight down but are now at a forty-five-degree angle, propped up by the bulk of the material.

"Ready for the bottom half?" BB inquires.

Before John Frederick can answer, a similarly bulky item appears at the edge of the screen. He slips it on with a smile. He can hear the lovely swishing sound of his thighs rubbing together as he moves his legs. He Velcros the two halves of his new outfit together and emerges from behind the screen.

BB claps his hands. "Marvelous, marvelous. Even better than I hoped. This is perhaps the best fat suit I have ever designed."

John Frederick looks at himself in the mirror, and then blushes. Even though he knows he is wearing a costume, for all intents and purposes, the image in the mirror is that of a very large and very naked John Frederick. He quickly grabs some clothing from the rack and returns to the shelter of the trifold screen.

Now decently covered, John Frederick again walks toward the mirror.

His image fills up exactly the right amount of space—no annoying margins of reflected chairs or walls surround him. His skin is once again filled with interesting mounds and hollows.

The wires of tension that have stretched around his neck, across his shoulders, and down his back begin to loosen.

"I'm back!" he shouts. "I know who I am! BB, you are a genius." John Frederick begins to dance around the room to the imagined strains of a Johann Strauss waltz. The fake flesh even jiggles! He knows, of course, that if this fat were real he could not fling himself about the room in this fashion—but it doesn't matter. For the first time in many months, he is truly at home in his skin.

⁘

Still happily padded, John Frederick climbs the stairs leading to his room. *How nice to be me again, yet still light and buoyant.* He remembers how his body used to shift ponderously from side to side as he negotiated the stairs, each step an exhausting challenge. He pauses at the doorway to his room, noticing how his body now barely fits through the doorway.

I must share this with someone, he decides. *I think I shall go downstairs and visit Mrs. Floyd.*

This time as he descends he gives an exaggerated hip thrust to one side and the fat suit sways appropriately, bringing a grin of delight to his face. He plods across the foyer to Mrs. Floyd's office and knocks gently on the door before entering.

Mrs. Floyd is sitting at her desk, her gaze directed downward at a stack of papers."

"Mr. Frederick," she says, raising her eyes. And then John Frederick is rewarded by a "Good . . . Oh my God," from Mrs. Floyd as she slips loosely from her chair onto the floor.

"Mrs. Floyd. Are you all right?" he asks softly as he moves to her side. Clearly his new look has made an impact.

⁘

John Frederick spends the next several hours in his new outerwear. The suit continues to calm and comfort him. "Almost like one of Lexie's pies in the good old days," he mutters. No, he must stop these periodic references to Lexie. She is gone, gone, gone. John Frederick feels the beginnings of anger and sadness, but then he pats his round, padded forearm and a sense of balance and right envelops him.

Chapter 34

A Night at the Theater

*J*ohn Frederick leans back into the soft tan leather seat of his chauffeured town car. The leather reminds him of his carefully packed expedition suitcase, now stowed in the trunk along with his fat suit, encased in its own protective garment bag. This is an historic day. John Frederick is about to embark on his first traveling day in over a year, which fills him with excitement—and, he must admit, not a little trepidation. Furthermore, he is traveling not on a culinary safari but on a much less caloric yet far more daring adventure. He is going into the city to see an actual live play. Familiar as he is with countless musicals, viewed repeatedly in his private screening room, this will be the first time John Frederick has seen such a production live.

When selecting the proper attire for this excursion, he originally omitted the fat suit; after all, wasn't it his former proportions that kept him from attending the theater in the first place? But just as he finished packing, he found himself returning to the closet to retrieve the bulk-enhancing garment. As he's told himself many times before, it doesn't hurt to be prepared.

◆•◆

John Frederick moves from the lobby into the main theater space and stops cold, overwhelmed by the realization that he is indeed in a real playhouse. He takes in the rows of seats filled with people (rather too many for his taste); the ornately carved proscenium arch; and, at the center of it all, the heavy red velour curtain protectively guarding the stage until the opening act.

"Your ticket, sir," requests a voice.

Stopped midworship, John Frederick registers that the black-suited usher has just repeated himself for the third time. John Frederick hands over the two perforated rectangles, trying to suppress the beginnings of an embarrassed flush.

"Fifth row center," the usher instructs. "Two on the aisle."

Settling into his designated seat, John Frederick is pleased that he took the precaution of purchasing a ticket for the adjacent space. Even with this breathing room, he is uncomfortably aware of the surrounding audience. A cacophony of voices, the scent of flowery cologne, and the odor of stale cigarette smoke clinging to the clothes of the person in front of him invade his senses. Then, suddenly, the houselights dim and the orchestra begins to tune.

John Frederick feels his whole body resonating with the instruments as they coalesce into one unified tone. His breath becomes one with the sound. Around him, the voices diminish, and John Frederick finds himself part of the collective anticipation sweeping across the theater. The orchestra launches into the overture, teasing John Frederick and his fellow listeners with bits and pieces of familiar tunes. And then it happens: the curtain begins to rise, and the latest revival of *The King and I* begins to weave its magic.

Despite having watched recorded versions of this same musical on numerous occasions, John Frederick feels as if he is watching the play for the first time. Everything is more vibrant, encompassing, and, well, *alive.* He hums along with music, joining the soft undercurrent of other muted participants throughout the audience. His only disappointment is that the king has a full head of hair rather than the traditional bald pate.

How Lexie would have enjoyed this. The thought rises unbidden into his consciousness. *If only she hadn't deserted me.* He can almost feel her presence in the supposedly empty seat beside him as the female lead sings "Hello, Young Lovers." However, any sense of sadness or longing is immediately vanquished by the King's musings over the puzzlements of the world, and the cheerful strains of "Getting to Know You."

All too soon, John Frederick is poised in front of his seat, clapping and shouting "Bravo" as the cast takes its curtain calls. It is, therefore, a happy but exhausted John Frederick who returns later that night to his first-class suite at the Hotel Grande. He quickly prepares for bed and then slips between the thousand-thread-count sheets, congratulating himself on leaving uneaten the Godiva chocolates that the staff has so graciously left on his pillow. *Lexie would be so proud*, he thinks as he drifts off to sleep.

John Frederick and Lexie face each other in the Grand Palace of the King of Siam. Lexie is wearing the most glorious of hoop skirts and her hair is pulled up into a twist of curls behind her head.

John Frederick bows. "May I have this dance?"

Lexie nods and moves toward him. He places one hand on her waist and with the other takes her small hand in his. They begin to dance and twirl across the floor.

◂•▸

The following morning John Frederick wakes left only with a fading vision of a wistful smile and a splash of red hair. He feels very sad.

On the way home, he wears his fat suit.

Chapter 35

Colors and Confrontations (Epiphany)

*T*he sky is blue and altogether too bright for John Frederick's mood. *What could be the problem?* he wonders. Nothing has felt right since his return from the theater.

Perhaps a walk would help. That this would be the first thing to pop into his mind is surely a sign of his distress. True, walking is no longer an ordeal, and at times is even pleasurable, but under normal circumstances it would be at least third or fourth on any list he might make of fun things to do. Perhaps Brunhilde inserted a mind-control device during one of her follow-up visits.

Despite this supposition, John Frederick heads for the great outdoors. However, just to make sure his free will has not been totally compromised, he decides to take a detour to the kitchen.

There is the usual moment of shock when he sees someone

of medium height, with decidedly nonred hair, and certainly not female, working at the stove. He quickly readjusts his vision.

"Good morning Mr. Frederick," says the non-Lexie.

"Good morning, Henri."

"I am cooking something special for you today. Would you care to have a taste?"

John Frederick takes the proffered spoon, tests the contents, and then, shaking his head, drops the spoon back into the pot. The splashing spoon sends a wave of liquid over the edge and onto the burner, where it sizzles and burns.

"Henri, this is inedible."

"You don't like it?"

"What do you think the word 'inedible' means? Are you illiterate as well as untalented?" As he speaks, John Frederick can feel the heat rising to his face. This is altogether too much.

He marches directly into Mrs. Floyd's office. "Mrs. Floyd, you must do something about Henri."

Mrs. Floyd says something under her breath. John Frederick cannot discern the actual words, but notices what appears to be an eye roll. No, he must be mistaken. Mrs. Floyd doesn't do eye rolls.

"What is wrong with that agency! This is the third unqualified chef in a row."

"Perhaps we might try offering an internship for a chef-in-training from L'Ecole Gastronomique."

"A totally inexperienced chef? That would be a disaster."

"But Mr. Frederick, Lexie had only just graduated and she was a definite success."

"Lexie was the exception that proves the rule. And don't forget, she ran out on us and left me in the lurch."

Mrs. Floyd straightens her shoulders and stares directly into John Frederick's eyes.

"John Frederick, I've held my tongue until now. After all, it is not my place to comment on your personal matters. But I must speak my mind. Lexie didn't desert you. You drove her away."

"That's impossible. I have always been the most reasonable of men. It was she who left me."

"But only because you treated her so abominably. You did nothing but yell, criticize, and accuse her of disloyalty."

"But…"

"And all that poor girl did was to support you and help you get healthy. Do you know she would stay up till all hours, researching ways to modify gourmet recipes so you wouldn't have to subsist on cottage cheese and carrot sticks?"

John Frederick sinks into the chair opposite Mrs. Floyd's desk. His legs feel as rubbery as when he first began walking after the heart attack. And indeed his heart does seem to be beating rather fast.

"I must go upstairs and rest."

❧•❧

Sitting on the edge of his bed, John Frederick ponders Mrs. Floyd's words. Unlike earlier, the view from the window seems to be in sync with his frame of mind: the beautiful blue sky is now partially obscured by drifting clouds that shift and change shape in a confusing pattern of dark and light.

"Can I really have been so terrible?" he asks the clouds.

John Frederick closes his eyes and hears the last words Lexie said to him: "I will not be treated this way any longer. I'll miss this place, I'll miss cooking and creating for you, and I'll even miss you. Or at least the old you. But no more of this. I quit."

This is followed immediately by a vision of him and Lexie sitting at the kitchen table, trading song titles and melodies.

John Frederick feels as if he has been looking at a painting through a small hole: before, all he could see is black and gray. But now the edges of the hole are beginning to expand, and he can see that the canvas also has broad streaks of color. Now there it is in all its complexity, an array of colors—bright, jumbled together, and yet somehow beautiful. The colors fill him with sadness and loss.

"Oh no," he cries. "What have I done?"

Chapter 36

Gingerbread Magic?

A cone of light surrounds Lexie's body as she kneads the dough that will later this morning become whole wheat sourdough rolls. The rest of Annie's Health Emporium is cloaked in an early-morning darkness that has not yet been broken by the slowly creeping light of the awakening day.

Lexie likes this feeling of illuminated solitude. It reminds her of that long-ago summer when her parents rented a house by the beach. Though her parents were disappointed by the unexpected fog, Lexie loved to walk through the soft gray mist where nothing existed outside her own body except the crunch of sand, the sound of the water ebbing and flowing over sand-embraced pebbles, and the salty smell of sea and floating kelp.

Lexie continues kneading. The movement of her flour-dusted fingers imitates the back-and-forth rhythm of that distant ocean, her fingers slowly synchronizing with her breath. She does not turn around when the silence is broken by the sound of the front door opening and the tapping of approaching footsteps.

"Hi, Annie," she calls, only vaguely registering that Annie rarely comes in the front door, preferring the back entrance nearest the parking lot.

"Hello, Lexie." The voice is hauntingly familiar but distinctly not Annie's.

Now Lexie turns and takes in the shape slowly emerging from the darkness. The face begins to form a recognizable pattern, and Lexie finds herself focusing on two brown eyes and a pair of soft, pale lips curved into a tentative smile. It is John Frederick—not the John Frederick of her nightmares or her last bleak days at Frederick House, but her old John Frederick, the one who sang her songs and cherished every morsel she created.

Lexie remembers the day they sang the whole score of *The King and I*. She wished at the time that they could waltz around the room like Anna and the King, but John Frederick's girth prevented any such movement. That Anna's hoop skirt was at least as voluminous as John Frederick's stomach, if not more, did not provide any consolation; the hoop skirt could be swept out of the way, unlike John Frederick's stomach.

Wait a minute, Lexie thinks. *There is no way John Frederick could be standing here, especially at this hour of the morning. I must still be at home, asleep.* Just to be sure, she pinches the web of skin between her thumb and forefinger with the nail and thumb of her other hand. Much to her surprise, it hurts. The John Frederick into whose eyes she is still staring is not a dream-induced apparition but an actual physical presence.

Lexie's gaze moves downward, only to discover that the aforementioned infamous stomach seems to have made its reappearance. Like her beloved John Frederick of old, the John Frederick who has entered Annie's Emporium is . . . *huge*. Were he to sit down at the counter, Lexie is sure that his weight would crush the bar stool—two bar stools, in fact.

Lexie's knees turn to quivering aspic, and she quickly leans against the counter, her hands splayed across the surface for support.

"Oh no," she cries, her head suddenly filled with the remembered sound of sirens, running feet, and the panting groans of the emergency medical team struggling down the stairs with their unconscious burden. Lexie knows that a replay is now inevitable.

A surge of anger breaks through the sorrow. All that effort, all that worry, the struggles, the verbal assaults, the loss of her new yellow room. All for nothing. Lexie can feel the blood rising to her face.

"Lexie, it's all right. It's just a fat suit," John Frederick says, pushing up a swaddled sleeve to reveal a forearm unencumbered by fat or foam. "It helps center me," he explains, "especially if I'm particularly anxious or afraid, or taking a great risk. Like now."

At least someone is centered, Lexie thinks, anger and sympathy warring inside her head. There is even a certain degree of admiration. The fat suit is such a clever John Frederickian solution.

"Lexie, I had to see you," John Frederick continues. "I know what I've done is unforgivable. I treated you so badly. It's just that I was so lost and adrift that everything turned into anger, and I used it against the one person who gave me nothing but support, caring, and friendship—you. That's not an excuse, but perhaps you can understand, just a little."

He reaches forward, his fingers stopping just a hair's breadth from Lexie's resting hand. She feels them nonetheless.

"I've done a lot of thinking and changing this past year," John Frederick says, "and now I'm picking up the pieces of my life. But there's a big piece missing—a piece called Alexandra Haynes."

Lexie takes a deep breath, ignoring the tears that are leaking out from behind her sense of self-assurance. It has taken so long for her to find her place in the world, a place where she is once more truly at home. If only John Frederick's insights had come months ago.

"I don't know," she says softly in response to his unspoken question. "I've been putting together the pieces of my life, too, and I don't know if there's a place in the pattern for a John Frederick."

"I understand," John Frederick says, "but please just think about it. Perhaps in time . . ." His voice trails off, and he slowly turns toward the front door. Lexie watches his large retreating back. "By the way," John Frederick adds wistfully, his hand on the doorknob, "the gingerbread smells great."

"Yes, it does," Lexie says to herself, listening to the jangling sound of the bell hanging from the front door and breathing in the scent of nutmeg, cloves, and ginger. She then reaches into her pocket, takes out her key ring, and moves from behind the counter to relock the door—but she finds it firmly locked. It is only then that she remembers that the bell made no sound earlier, and that she is not making gingerbread but vinegary-smelling sourdough rolls.

Chapter 37

The Myth of Good Things and Small Packages

*J*ohn Frederick walks down the path, the breeze blowing cool air against his skin. He can also feel a hint of warmth, as if the weather were reluctant to begin its descent into the cold of winter. *Even the weather doesn't like change*, he thinks to himself, although he knows all too well that change is inevitable.

He turns toward his walking companion. "I saw Lexie last week."

Caleb Mayfield looks faintly surprised. "How's she doing?" he asks. "I haven't talked to her in quite awhile. We used to talk a lot. You know, I helped her settle in when she . . . er . . . left Frederick House."

"Yes, I know," John Frederick says. "I'm glad she had a friend." To his surprise he realizes he actually means it.

"I thought at one time it might turn into something more, but . . . ," Caleb's voice trails off.

John Frederick stops himself from saying "I'm glad" once again. Instead he ponders the beautiful power of the word "but." Like the rotating platform at the end of a trolley line, "but" turns the sentence completely around so that it is now heading in the opposite direction. Finally answering Caleb's original question, he says out loud, "She's doing well. Still cooking, of course."

John Frederick takes in Caleb's nod, and the two continue back toward the house in a silence which, if not exactly companionable, is certainly far from uncomfortable.

　　　　　　　　━ ● ━

"There's a package for you. It's marked personal," Mrs. Floyd calls out as John Frederick and Caleb enter the room. "I've put it on the table."

"Thank you. I'll get to it in a moment."

Caleb turns toward John Frederick. "I've got to be going anyway. If I leave right now I just might beat the traffic back to the city. Thanks for the walk."

John Frederick moves across the now-silent room, his attention focused on the plain brown paper-wrapped parcel sitting on the table. There is no return address or postmark, nothing except his name and a series of prestamped phrases—"PERSONAL," "HANDLE WITH CARE," and "THIS SIDE UP"—printed on the top and sides of the box. Despite its anonymity, John Frederick somehow feels sure the package poses no physical threat.

Taking the scissors Mrs. Floyd has thoughtfully placed next to the package, John Frederick begins to peel away the heavy brown wrapping paper. Underneath is a smaller cardboard box, also plain and unlabeled. He carefully cuts through the sealing tape. The box is filled with green and white packing peanuts, and the smell of something both comforting and disturbing. As John Frederick reaches inside, the displaced packing peanuts cascade over the sides of the box and hit the table in soft, puffy bounces. He can feel the edge of yet another box. Slowly, he begins to pull the box toward him.

＊·＊

Mrs. Floyd, alarmed by the sounds emanating from beyond her office, opens the door and moves cautiously into the other room. John Frederick is sitting at the table, head bowed into his hands, which are resting on what looks like a pile of green-and-white snow. Beside him is a small pink box, which has been opened to reveal the most perfect, moist piece of gingerbread that Mrs. Floyd has ever seen. A piece of notepaper rests beside it, the contents undecipherable from where she is standing.

She notices John Frederick's shoulders as they heave up and down, shaking his whole body, accompanied by the loud "whuh, whuh" sound that originally drew her attention.

Mrs. Floyd cannot tell if he is laughing or crying.

Acknowledgments

I would like to thank my teacher and mentor Linda Schreyer, who encouraged me to write fiction again and was there supporting me every step of the way; Paula Bernstein my writing buddy and compassionate critic who talked me back from the edge more than once; Jenna Sugarman, who edited my first "final" draft; Krissa Lagos, who did the final editing; and Brooke Warner, Caitlyn Levin, and the staff at She Writes Press who transformed my manuscript into a published book. I would also like to thank my fellow writing retreat participants, especially Erica di Bono, Darlene Basch and Jackie Peterson, for their insights, critiques and companionship.

Finally, I want to express my appreciation to Mr. Wondra, Ms. Keating and all the teachers and librarians who shared with me their passion for writing, composition, and the beauty of the English language.

About the Author

Julie Franken

*C*athryn Novak has had a years-long love affair with words that began as soon as she could read. After graduating with a degree in communications and public policy from UC Berkeley, Cathryn did a stint in advertising before devoting the rest of her professional career to public service. During that period she wore many hats, including speech writer, policy analyst, and investigative report writer. Her monograph on the Los Angeles Police Commission, *The Years of Controversy*, was published by the Police Foundation in Washington, DC. Now retired, Cathryn has returned to her first love: the world of fiction. *Size Matters* is her first published novel.

CPSIA information can be obtained
at www.ICGtesting.com
Printed in the USA
FSOW02n1416280816
24278FS